"That was quite an experience," Killian said dreamily

She was sitting facing Gus in the bathtub.

"What was?" he asked, massaging her legs.

"Making love in the hayloft." She tipped her head back, reminiscing Gus's expert lovemaking.

"Taking a roll in the hay, you mean," he said, a grin nudging the corners of his mouth.

"I suppose it's old hat to you—rolling in the hay, taking a bath with a woman, giving her a massage. . . ."

"Sure," he confirmed teasingly. "I do it every day. It's my moonlighting job. I usually charge a grand for such services, but you're special. I'll only charge you a hundred."

"Gee, thanks," she murmured, her eyes still closed.

"You remember that film . . . *American Gi*_____ *____* I'm the Oklahoma Gi_____ose.

Sh_____ inute she saw da_____ new he meant bu_____ e whispered.

"I play to win . . . and I'm out to win you."

Delayne Camp found inspiration for *Oklahoma Man* when she read an article in the newspaper about film wranglers—people with unique skills who train animals to perform stunts in movies. Delayne was also fascinated by the cowboy figure, and though she herself lives in a city, she says she can appreciate the unique contribution of cowboys "not only to the fabric of our country, but to women's fantasies." Certainly the hero in *Oklahoma Man* is one superb fantasy!

Delayne has written over thirty novels and is also published under the pen names Elaine Camp, Deborah Camp and Deborah Benet.

Oklahoma Man
DELAYNE CAMP

Harlequin Books

TORONTO • NEW YORK • LONDON
AMSTERDAM • PARIS • SYDNEY • HAMBURG
STOCKHOLM • ATHENS • TOKYO • MILAN

Published February 1991

ISBN 0-373-25435-0

OKLAHOMA MAN

1

APPLYING THE BRAKES as she steered the car into another hairpin turn, Killian Whittier sucked in her breath and sent up a prayer when the tires squealed on the wet pavement and the car fishtailed. As it slowed to under twenty miles an hour, the car still had trouble rounding the bend and Killian knew she wouldn't make her destination that night. The rainstorm was winning, sapping her energy and setting her nerves on edge. She glimpsed the blur of red neon ahead and tried to read the sign through the rain-streaked windshield.

M...O...T...

That's all she needed to see. Killian guided the gold El Dorado onto the asphalt strip next to the entrance of the motel. She switched off the engine and rested her forehead on crossed wrists against the steering wheel. Her muscles relaxed, one by one.

Safe, she told herself. Spend the night here, get some sleep and tomorrow it won't be raining buckets or crackling lightning. In fact, it'll probably be a beautiful, sunny day. Like native son Will Rogers used to say—if you don't like the weather in Oklahoma, just wait a minute.

Composed once again, Killian drew the hood of her black slicker over her blond hair and grabbed her tube-shaped bag. She dashed from her car to the motel carport, leaping over puddles and diving under the sheltering overhang. She ran a hand down her face, flinging off raindrops and feeling the dampness seep into her bones. Killian pushed against the heavy glass door and stumbled into the lobby.

It was decorated in soothing blues and grays. Her boots left damp tracks on the carpet. The young man behind the registration desk sent her a sympathetic smile.

Another man, tall and broad-shouldered, stood nearby and dripped onto the carpet, making Killian feel right at home. His rawhide jacket bore wet dots and his black boots were water-spotted and muddy. His cowboy hat, riding low on his forehead, shadowed his face so that she couldn't make out his features. She wondered if he was as relieved as she to have found a dry dock in that raging sea outside.

"Looks like you got a little damp," the motel clerk said by way of a greeting.

"Just a little," Killian agreed, laying her hands flat on the desk as she imagined the comfort of a warm bed. "I'd like a room, please."

"I hate to tell you this—" the clerk shrugged, hands turning palms up, "—but you're five minutes too late. I just rented the last available room."

Killian felt the blood drain from her face. If only she could faint, the clerk would have to let her lie down. "You're kidding me. How many rooms do you have here?" She glanced around. The place couldn't be that popular. "You can't be full."

"I'm terribly sorry," the clerk said. "It's a busy week-end. One-hundred-and-seventy-five hairstylists checked in this morning for a convention." His gaze slid to the man in the cowboy hat, who was flipping through a display of postcards. "And just a few minutes before you came in, this gentleman took the last room we had available. Sorry." He shrugged again and offered an insipid smile. "Nothing I can do about it, I'm afraid. There's another motel about twenty or thirty miles up the—"

"Oh, no." Killian groaned as she retrieved her duffle bag. "I'd rather sleep in the car than have to drive another foot in this deluge. My tires are slick even when the roads aren't, so I'll stay put until this rain lets up, thank you very much."

"Ma'am?"

She half turned toward the other man. Lucky devil, she thought, lifting an eyebrow to let him know she'd heard him and was waiting to hear what he had to say. He had a room and she didn't, so she decided she didn't like him.

"I won't let you sleep out in your car when I can do something about it," he said in an Oklahoma drawl that coaxed a smile from her. Pulling a gold key ring from his back pocket, he tossed it onto the desk. "You can have the room and I'll sleep outside."

Killian reassessed her decision. Funny how dislike can suddenly turn to profound admiration. The shadow cast by the brim of his hat inched up to reveal a stubbly square chin. His lower lip was full and moist. Killian wanted to bend her knees and look up under his hat, but she didn't dare.

"I have a trailer out there." He tipped his head toward the entrance. "I've slept many a night in it. It's right comfortable."

"I should tell you that I wouldn't hear of it," Killian said, trying on a beguiling smile. "But the words seem to be sticking in my throat."

He chuckled—a breathy, growling staccato that set off a shiver along Killian's spine. Sweeping the midnight-blue hat from his head, he revealed himself to her at last. Thick, curly black hair, liberally shot through with silver, tumbled to his forehead and over the tops of his ears. He pushed the fingers of one hand through his hair, combing it back and lifting it off his skull where the hat had flattened it. Killian was relieved to see that he was older than her thirty years, but not too much older. He was prematurely gray, and she liked that about him.

His earthy brown eyes were fringed by dark lashes and accentuated by the bold slashes of his black eyebrows. A smile tugged his mouth—a lush mouth—and dimples made shallow impressions in his lean cheeks. All in all, he was fine-looking, not unlike big movie stars. But this was no imitation cowboy. His sunburned hands were wide and lightly scarred on the backs. Square-tipped fingers danced along the brim of the hat he held, displaying the agility and surety it takes to rein a horse with one hand and twirl a rope with the other.

His polite appraisal of her took on a more personal attitude as his gaze moved up her body, pausing ever so slightly on the damp shirt outlining the curves of her breasts. When his eyes met hers, she saw attraction lurking in them.

"Take the room," he insisted. "This'll give me a chance to show off the manners my Mama taught me."

His charm made her feel warm all over. She smiled, felt her cheeks blush, and took the key. The pleased clerk pushed a white registration card forward and held out a pen for her.

"Thank you," she murmured, feeling shy under the cowboy's intense gaze. "You're very kind."

"You're welcome," he said, leaning closer to read the name she'd written at the top of the card. "Killian Whittier."

He smelled of lime and damp leather. He grinned when she circled the "Ms." on the card and pulled back to give her breathing room.

"*Ms.* Killian Whittier," he amended. "As in unattached?"

"Exactly." She sent him a sidelong glance. "What about you—married, engaged, living with?"

"None of the above." He held out his hand. "My name's Gus. It's a pleasure and it's all mine."

"Not entirely," she said, having finished filling out the motel registration and half turning to shake his hand. She pushed back the hood of her slicker. She liked the way a smile nudged his mouth into a shy grin.

"A blonde," he noted, lifting his eyebrows. "The last blonde who bumped up against me was from New York and thought the rodeo was a street in California."

"Not this blonde," Killian said with a laugh as she glanced at the room number on the brass key. Number seventy-seven. Was this her lucky day or what? "I'm an Oklahoman, through and through. I cut my teeth on tornadoes, oil rigs and hand-tooled leather."

"There you go," he drawled, fitting his hat back onto his head and looking past her to the driving rain.

"Are you sure you'll be all right out there?" Killian asked, turning toward the glass doors. "The weather forced me off the highway."

"Me, too. My trailer kept trying to jackknife on me." He winked at her in a reassuring way. "But I'll be fine. Just fine. There is one thing you can do for me."

"Name it."

"Meet me in the restaurant for dinner." He slung a suit carrier over his shoulder and tucked his shaving kit under the other arm. "Will an hour give you enough time to dry off?"

Appreciating his take-charge attitude, she nodded. "Meet you in an hour," she promised, already walking away. "And thanks again. You saved my life."

He waited until she was out of earshot before he added, "And what a nice life to save." His comment drew an agreeable chuckle from the desk clerk, reminding Gus that he wasn't alone. "Well, back outside for me, partner."

"I'm sorry, sir," the clerk said.

Gus grinned, thinking of his dinner date. Summerblond, blue-eyed, husky-voiced and curvy-slender, she represented what he always thought was the ideal woman. "I'm not sorry," he said, feeling like a tomcat on the prowl. "I'm not one bit sorry."

HE SAW HER STANDING NEAR the entrance to the restaurant, one hand fiddling with a thin, gold chain around her neck, the other clutching a white purse. Gus held back, enjoying the view and telling himself that he was a lucky son-of-a-gun to have run into her. He wasn't usually superstitious, but he couldn't help thinking he was destined to meet her. After all, he'd never felt such a strong attraction for a woman so suddenly. Not just a physical attraction, he mused, but a down-deep elation.

He'd taken pains in dressing, although doing so in the cramped trailer hadn't been easy. Wishing he'd brought along something flashy to wear, he'd had to settle for Levi's and a clean, white shirt with pearl snap buttons. He'd managed to spit-shine his boots, removing the mud and water spots. But looking at her made him feel as if he'd been dressed at a church rummage sale.

She'd parted her hair on the side and it fell to her shoulders in a straight, blunt cut. Wispy strands touched her golden eyebrows and lent allure to her eyes, which were a rare shade of blue-green. Her nails were unpolished and short, so he figured she worked with her hands. A woman of action, he thought. Not a giggly gaggle of blond curls and batting eyelashes.

He hooked his thumbs in the front pockets of his jeans, dazed at his good luck. The storm had brought more than just an ill-wind his way, he thought. His gaze drifted over her lemon-yellow shirt and green twill slacks. She wore heels, but she was still four or five inches shorter than him. He started forward just as she turned his way. His heartbeat quickened when her lips curved into a luscious flirtatious smile.

"Don't you look larrupin'," he said, speaking his mind a little hastily.

"My, my. You sound like a man with an appetite." Her jewel-like eyes widened, then she looked into the restaurant and nodded toward a far corner. "There's a table for two over there with our name on it. Shall we?"

"After you," he said, extending a hand and feeling like a damn fool for coming on like a starving beast. He hung back to admire the gentle sway of her hips in the snug trousers and the nip of her waist. He feasted his eyes on her, and realized he couldn't get enough of looking at her.

Gus held out a chair for her before seating himself in the other. A votive candle threw a soft, golden light on her face. She picked up her menu, blocking the enchantment of her face from his view. With a resigned sigh Gus studied his own menu, made a quick decision, and handed the menu over to the waiter who had stopped at their table.

"Want something to drink, Killian?"

"Yes, please. Would you care to share a carafe of Chablis?"

"Sounds good," he agreed. "I'm going to have the sirloin, medium rare. What about you?"

"I'll try the chicken fettuccini with a dinner salad and house dressing," she said with a smile, while Gus observed her. She had tiny moles near the corners of her eyes, teardrop-shaped. Fascinating woman, he thought.

"How's the room?" he asked after the waiter had left.

"Very dry and very warm," she said, with a husky laugh. She looked around before leaning closer as if she was about to share a secret thought with him. "Isn't this strange? Talk about standing out like sore thumbs!"

"What are you talking about?"

"The other people," she whispered urgently. "The hairstylists in here. Remember, the clerk said there was a convention? Almost everyone in this room has some strange kind of hairstyle. That woman to our left . . . her hair is navy blue! And look at the man seated with her. Doesn't his haircut make you think of a cock's comb?"

Gus forced his gaze away from her lips and looked at the other diners. Sure as shootin', they were a strange collection. He felt as though he were in a science fiction movie.

"Well, I'll be." He laughed under his breath. "I hadn't noticed."

"How could you not?"

He smiled briefly and dropped his gaze from hers. "I guess I only have eyes for you."

She released a breathy laugh and sat back in her chair, shaking her head at him and making her hair swing alluringly. "You just come out and say the most corny things, don't you?"

"Yes." He winced at what he was about to say. "And what's really awful is that I mean them."

They looked at each other, fascinated—a moment of magic only broken by the appearance of the waiter, who had brought the carafe.

Killian looked past Gus's right shoulder to the window and the rain outside. She pretended to study it while she was really exploring her reaction to the man in the blindingly white, western cut shirt. Was he playing games with her? That's how she felt. Secure one moment and then sent into orbit the next.

I only have eyes for you . . . She felt the smile in her heart, but wouldn't let it claim her lips, fearing he'd ask her why she was smiling and she might be tempted to tell him: you make me smile, Gus. You make me feel so many things I haven't felt in a long time.

She realized she was staring at a black pickup truck to which was attached a long, red horse trailer. It sat under a light pole and raindrops jumped off the truck hood, no doubt making a racket. *Probably sounds like machine-gun fire inside that trailer*, she thought. The trailer shifted, causing rivulets to cascade over the side of it. Killian sharpened her gaze, noticing that the trailer wasn't empty as she'd assumed.

"What's wrong?" Gus asked, twisting around to see what had captured her attention.

"There's a horse out there in that trailer," Killian explained. "And I bet the rain is noisy on that roof, don't you? Poor thing."

"It is noisy," he agreed, turning back to her. "But nothing much bothers Apache. I imagine he's sound asleep."

"You mean, that's *your* trailer. . ." Killian stared at him, her eyes wide open as she realized just how much he'd given up for her. "A horse trailer," she said, her voice reflecting her chagrin. "I thought you meant you'd be sleeping in a travel trailer or I would never have taken your room!"

He laughed briefly at her horror, glancing away for a moment to survey the room and its odd occupants before his eyes swept to her again. He crossed his arms on the table and leaned toward her. "Don't worry about it," he said in a near whisper. "That thing is a travel trailer to me. I've got a sleeping bag in it just as comfy as can be."

"But there's a horse in there with you!"

"So? Horses are good company." He sat back, hooking one elbow over the back of his chair. "Don't look so guilt-ridden. Believe me, I'm used to sleeping in proximity to horses. Apache and me are good buddies."

"Well..." She shrugged helplessly. "I guess there's nothing I can do unless I give the room back to you—" her smile was mischievous "—and I'm not about to be that magnanimous."

The waiter brought their salads and refilled their wineglasses before moving to another table. Gus fingered the dinner knife, sliding his fingertips up and down to feel the design of rosebuds and climbing vines on its handle as naughty thoughts flowered within him. When his eyes met Killian's again, she froze, losing interest in the salad. Obviously he was more transparent than he thought.

"The only other alternative would be to share the room with me," he suggested teasingly, with a grin on his face. He made a face, wrinkling his nose and flashing white teeth. "I know, I know," he said stopping her before she could set him straight. "You're not that obliging, right?"

"Right." She matched him smile for smile, then attacked her salad. When she was certain her heart rate had slowed and she had regained her composure, she continued. "Do you live around here?" She was proud of herself for sounding so casual, even indifferent, when she was all atremble inside. Sharing a room with him . . . get that out of your poor, depraved mind, Killian! He was joking.

"Not too far away. I've got a place outside Porter. You know where that is?"

"Sure!" She forced herself not to jump up and down for pure joy. "Porter's the peach capital of Oklahoma. I live in Broken Arrow, so we're practically neighbors."

"We sure are," he agreed, running a hand down the front of his cotton shirt, his fingertips skimming over the pearlized snaps. Whoa, boy, he told himself. Don't make a bigger fool of yourself by giving a whoop and a holler just because the lady lives near you. Besides, you know you'd drive clear to the moon if only to see her again. "What do you do for a living?"

"I'm a veterinarian. What about you? I bet you raise horses, don't you?"

"You'd win that bet." He looked at her hands again seeing them as a doctor's hands. Gentle, strong, clean of line. "Quarter horses mostly, with a few Morgans and Arabians thrown in for fun."

"That sounds like paradise to me," she said, and her admission was heartfelt.

Gus looked down at his empty salad bowl. When had he eaten the salad? He hadn't tasted a thing. He noticed that hers was empty, too, but couldn't remember seeing her take one bite. The waiter came with their dinners, and Gus ate in silence, dividing his attention between the meal and his comely dinner date. He fancied that the other men in the room looked his way with envy. Even the waiter seemed smitten, hovering nearby to refill Killian's wine and waterglasses and twist fresh pepper onto her fettuccini. When she asked him to extend her compliments to the chef, the mustachioed man acted as if she'd told him he looked like Clark Gable's double. Blushing to the tops of his ears, the waiter hurried to the kitchen with the good news.

"Is your practice in Broken Arrow?" Gus asked, forcing himself to concentrate a little more on the food this time. The woman had him bewitched, pure and simple.

"Yes. Actually, I co-own it with my father. Maplewood Clinic."

"I've heard of it," he said. "It's in that shopping center near the expressway."

"That's the one. Which vet do you use? Brandenburg?" she asked, naming the most prominent horse doctor in the county.

"Sometimes I use Brandenburg, but most of the time I use myself. I'm pretty good at making sick horses well." He gave a shrug, not wanting to take anything from her. "No formal training, but since I've been around horses all my life, I've got a few tricks up my sleeve."

"I just bet you have," she murmured, delivering a provocative smile that made his blood sing. Killian stared at her plate. Had she actually said that? *You're crazy*, she told herself, *and you're tempting fate.* Don't challenge the devil unless you're ready to pay his due. She waved her fork to signal a change in the subject. "I have a few acres in Broken Arrow. I hope to have more property some day."

"What for? Do you want to raise cattle or horses?"

"Actually, I want to provide a shelter for animals who need a home. Mistreated animals, abandoned animals. It infuriates me when I hear about horses and cattle that have been starved or beaten. It happens too often and there aren't many places where they can stay to recuperate."

He nodded, frowning at a memory she'd evoked. "Like those poor horses that were ridden to death a few weeks ago. Did you read about that?"

"Yes, an endurance race," she added. "The owners should be made to run around a dirt track in the hot sun until *they* drop." She took a deep breath, relieving some of her pent-up anger. Why was it so hard for her to find a neutral topic? She was either blatantly flirting with him or lecturing him! "Incidents such as those are the reason I got involved in working with animal protection agencies," she said somewhat lamely since she was convinced he was ready to call it a night.

"Oh, really? What kind of work do you do for them? Free veterinary services?"

"No. My father does some of that, but I investigate cruelty cases."

"Good for you." He brought his hand down on the table for emphasis and almost upset the wineglasses. *Idiot*, he branded himself, then tried to compensate his emphatic gesture by adding, "Somebody should keep an eye out for the helpless beasts."

"That's what brings me out in this storm," Killian explained. Was she babbling? It sounded that way to her. The poor cowboy across from her probably wished she'd just say good-night and end this performance. She intended to do just that, but heard herself saying instead, "I'm headed for Bartlesville."

"No kidding? That's where I'm going, too." He chuckled, warmed by her smile and the wine. Probably should tell her good-night so she could make a graceful escape, he thought. She was most likely bored stiff. But he couldn't end the evening just yet. Not when she was making his heart dissolve into a puddle in his chest. "It's a small world and my lucky day. Maybe I'll see you around Bartlesville. How long will you be staying?"

"It depends on how long my investigation will take to complete." She tipped her head to one side to puzzle something out. "I thought you said you lived in Porter."

"I do." He chuckled, intrigued by her every movement. He was falling hard for this woman. "I'm working in Bartlesville." He paused, wanting to inject drama into the moment. His occupation never failed to spark interest. It seemed that everybody loved to hear about the film business. "A movie's being shot there and I'm the boss wrangler."

"You . . . boss wrangler?"

He took her confusion for a lack of show business knowledge. "Right. The movie's a Western and that means it needs horses and somebody who knows about horses. A boss wrangler provides the stock and matches the mounts with the actors. I train Hollywood horses," he said, amused by her wide eyes and slack mouth. "That means I teach them to fall, roll over, rear up—all on cue. And I make sure the animals are all taken care of and not abused in any way, shape or form. There's also an animal rights person on hand, just to make sure things are kept on the up-and-up. You'll be pleased to know that we follow strict—"

"Gus," she said, interrupting him. "Are you *August* Breedlove?" She shook her head, denying her intuition and the facts staring her in the face. "You're not." She saw the answer in his eyes and her heart nose-dived. "You are. You *are* August Breedlove."

It was his turn to stare at her. "That's right. How did you know? Does my reputation precede me?"

"Gus..." She shook her head, unable to find a way out of the trap she'd fallen into. Finally she grabbed her glass of wine and drank it. Then she faced Gus with stone-cold sobriety. "I'm going to Bartlesville to investigate reports of animal cruelty on the movie set. Surely, you're aware of the accusations."

"Say *what?*" he shouted.

Her revelation had made him shoot up from the chair like a rocket. Hands balled at his sides and his breath coming in short, scorching gasps, he forced himself to sit down again and lower his voice to an acceptable level.

"I don't know what the hell you're talking about," he said between clenched teeth. "There's obviously some mistake."

"How long have you been away from the set?"

"Three days."

"Who's been in charge while you've been away?"

"My nephew," he said, his tone daring her to question the integrity of his kin. "I trained the boy myself."

"I got a call yesterday from the animal rights rep on the set," Killian explained, keeping her voice steady. "She said there was evidence that a trip-wire had been used in a scene where a horse is supposed to be shot from under the rider."

"That's impossible," he asserted, falling back in the chair in utter disgust.

"That's why I'm going to Bartlesville," she said, calm in the face of his storm. "If it's impossible, then I'll be the first to report there's been a mistake."

"I don't believe this." He brought a fist down on the table, making the flatware and glasses shudder. "I'm away for three lousy days and all hell breaks loose." He pointed a finger at her, angry that she'd changed from a princess to a shrew right before his eyes. "I'll tell you one damned thing. You're being lied to, lady. Ask anybody. August Breedlove has a spotless reputation and—"

"I know that," she said softly. "That's why this is so serious and why I was called in as a special investigator. Gus . . ." She reached across the table and rested her cool hand on one of his hot fists. *Don't look at me as if I'm a two-headed monster! I didn't arrange this farce, you know.* "Don't take this personally. I'm sure there's a logical—"

Gus snatched his fist from under her hand and stood up, so humiliated he felt physically ill. He shook his head when she started to console him again, unable to take her pity, her voice of reason. A man was only as good as his reputation and she'd just thrown mud on his!

"Save it," he snapped at her, then grabbed up the check. "I don't want your pretty, empty words. I hope you have a taste for crow because that's what you'll be eating once you get to Bartlesville. See you there."

Before she could muster a comeback, he pivoted sharply and strode toward the front of the restaurant, paid the bill, then marched out into the rain.

Killian stared after him, too stunned to move. After a full minute of feeling numb, she blinked and looked around. Faces beneath wild hairdos stared back at her. Flinging her napkin onto the table, she stood up and left the restaurant, feeling strangely conspicuous in a room chock-full of oddities. She went to her room, slammed the door behind her and threw herself onto the bed.

August Breedlove, she thought with a moan. Of all the men in the world . . . and of all the little motels in Oklahoma . . . why did *he* have to show up at this one?

"And he was so perfect," she said, mentally cursing her bad luck. "Mr. Right if ever there was one!"

But that didn't amount to a hill of beans now. She'd investigated quite a few cruelty cases and had never made any close friends after she'd ferreted out the truth. People weren't usually mean, but they were always glad to see the last of her. Gus would be no different. He'd already drawn the battle lines.

She pulled her duffle bag onto the bed with her and extracted a folder from inside it. Examining the notes she'd taken before heading for Bartlesville, she mulled over what the president of the wrangler association had said about the accused.

"Breedlove would never approve of such a thing," the man had insisted. "You've been hoodwinked, honey."

Hope so, she thought, flipping to the next page of notes she'd taken while talking to a movie director who'd worked with Breedlove.

"He's the best," the director had told her. "He treats his animals better than I treat my actors. Has to be some kind of mistake."

Has to be, she agreed, recalling Gus's teasing grin and raspy chuckle. She closed the folder, fascinated by the thought of how much she liked him.

It wasn't natural for her to trust a man so quickly. When he'd told her he was single, she'd believed him. Just like that! If any other man had told her that in the lobby of a motel, she would have been instantly suspicious, cautious. But Gus had honest eyes. Dark, earthy, honest eyes.

With a burst of frustration, she shoved the folder back into the duffle and flung the bag into a nearby chair.

"Why does this have to happen to me?" she asked venting her anger by slamming her fists several times into the soft mattress. Gus was probably dreading tomorrow as much as she was, she thought. Dreading the next confrontation when she would play investigator. But the animal rights activist had been positive there'd been foul play.

"Just wait until you examine the horse," she'd told Killian over the phone. "It was a trip-wire. I'll stake my job on it."

Strong words, Killian thought, cringing at the predicament Gus had been placed in. Usually she was worried about the animal that had been mistreated, but not this time. This time she worried about the man sleeping outside in a horse trailer. Out in the cold, pouring rain.

2

IT WAS EASY TO SPOT the film's director. He wore a baseball cap and a T-shirt advertising films he'd worked on. Bearded, bespectacled and full of himself, he paid little attention to Killian as she approached. In fact his body language said it all—*I am somebody and you're not, so keep your distance.*

Upon arriving at the movie location, Killian had been greeted by the animal rights representative. She'd been told that the director wanted to see her right away. After asking a few crew members for directions, she'd finally located the hub of activity out by a rickety barn built just for the movie. It looked as if it were a hundred years old, but it was probably only a hundred days old, Killian thought.

"Jerry Bishop?" Killian asked, breaching the invisible wall the director had erected around himself. "Excuse me, but you *are* Jerry—"

"Tom," the baseball-capped man said, glaring at the aide by his elbow, "see to this girl." With that, he went back to studying the storyboard.

Tamping down her temper, Killian smiled at Tom and shook her head slightly to put him off. Then she committed the unpardonable sin of touching the director's arm. He spun around, his eyes flashing warning signals. Tom lurched forward to contain her.

"Young woman, please!" The director glared at her hand on his arm. "Tom, get her out—"

"I assume you're Jerry Bishop," Killian interrupted. "I've been sent to investigate allegations of cruelty to animals on this set."

That got his attention, all right. In the blink of an eye Tom backed off and Jerry Bishop changed from a growling beast to a purring pussycat. Instead of peeling her fingers off his arm, one by one, he patted her hand and pressed it more firmly onto his forearm.

"Yes, I'm Jerry." He tried to win her with his smile—a blaze of flashing white teeth amid his curly, marbled beard and mustache. "And what's your name, dear?"

"Killian Whittier," she said, tugging her hand out from beneath his and then extending it in a polite, civilized manner. "I don't mean to interrupt, but I was told you wanted to see me right away."

"That's right." He shook her hand and smiled again— an expansive I'm-your-best-friend smile. "Killian, you've got a movie star's name and a movie star's looks."

She smiled back—a small, tight, cut-the-bull smile. "I'd like to see the injured horse, please. Where is it being stabled?"

"You need to meet our boss wrangler. Once you meet him, you'll see how absurd this whole business is. August Breedlove wouldn't hurt—"

"I've met him."

"—a fly," he finished, then stared at her as his mouth dropped open. "You've met him already? You mean, in a professional setting? You've investigated—"

"Yes, last night. And no, not professionally—no, I've never investigated his practices." She laughed at the stumbling conversation. "Let's start again," she suggested. "I had the good fortune of meeting Mr. Breedlove last night. The storm stranded us at the same motel." She shrugged, thinking how convenient it all sounded. "It's a small world, especially in Oklahoma. Anyway, yes, we've met. Furthermore, I've heard only good things about Mr. Breedlove's treatment of animals. However, I still would like to see the horse in question, if you'd be so kind."

Jerry tried another of his seductive smiles on her and leaned closer, treating her to a wink. "You're not going to make our lives miserable, are you, honey?"

"The horse, Mr. Bishop," Killian said, resenting his attempt to pull her into a conspirator's role. "May I see it, please?"

Jerry Bishop snatched the cap off his head and ran a hand over his shining pate. He looked toward the barn to a grouping of horses and men, then raised a megaphone to his mouth. Killian realized that one of the men in cowboy hats was Gus. He seemed to be checking the belly strap on one of the mounts.

"Breedlove, get over here. The *law* wants you."

Every head turned in their direction, making Killian fight an urge to kick Jerry Bishop in the seat of his stonewashed jeans. She cut him down to size with a sharp glance.

"That was uncalled for, not to mention appallingly immature and unprofessional," she said, aware that having insulted him, she'd made him her sworn enemy in only a few seconds.

"Sorry, hon, but I've got a film to make and every minute I waste with you costs me thousands of dollars." He stepped in front of Killian, giving her an up-close-and-personal view of the back of his blue T-shirt. "Gus, that woman from the humane society is here to hassle you," he said as Gus Breedlove came within earshot. "Take care of her. She's *your* headache, not mine."

Something squeezed Killian's heart as her eyes met Gus's. He looked magnificent as the bright sunshine lightened his eyes to cinnamon and highlighted the silver strands in his hair. Jeans, pale blue from many washings, hugged his hips and long legs. Boots, scraped by spurs and thorny bushes, added an inch to his already impressive height. Anger, pent-up and burning white-hot, pulled down the corners of his sensuous mouth and made a muscle jerk below his left ear. Although she reckoned he was still angry with her, she knew he was fighting mad at Jerry Bishop for embarrassing him in front of everyone.

"Bishop, I've got just one thing to say to you before I take this lady to the stables," Gus said, his voice pitched dangerously low. He stripped off his work gloves, then slapped them into his palm as he locked gazes with the director. "If you keep on treating me like a lackey, I'm going to rebel all over your face." With that, he cupped Killian's elbow in his warm hand and guided her away toward the stables.

Biting her lower lip to keep from laughing aloud at Jerry Bishop's stunned expression, Killian switched her attention to the man walking briskly at her side. His iron jawline told her he was steaming inside, and she loved him for controlling his temper sufficiently enough to set Bishop straight on the law of muscle over bravado.

"It's good to see you, Gus, and I'm glad you put Bishop in his place."

He dismissed the whole scene with a shrug. "I don't like that guy."

"I don't know him but my first impression isn't—"

"The stables are over there," he interrupted, pointing ahead to a farmhouse and a long building stretching out behind it. "Gold Dollar has been treated, but you're welcome to look him over. I'll leave you to your business and—"

"Gus, do we have to be adversaries?" Killian asked, cutting into his curt statements. "Believe me, I'm used to being persona non grata around movie sets, but I was hoping we could work together without hostility. Last night was so friendly...so—"

"That was before I knew you were out to get me," he snapped, then heaved a quick sigh of regret.

She stopped to examine his hangdog expression with concern. Resting a hand on his arm, she made him look into her eyes. "I'm not out to get anybody. Are you going to fight me every inch of the way? Won't you cooperate?"

"I thought I was." He propped his hands at his fancy-stitched belt. Sunlight reflected off the big, silver buckle and almost blinded her. "Look, I've got a million and one things to do today, so do you mind if we crank this errand into fast-forward?"

"Fine," she bit out, irritated with him. She marched on toward the long building, leaving him to follow in her wake.

Once she'd entered the stables she felt on more solid ground. The familiar smell of horses and hay was heaven to her and the cool, dust-moted interior felt just like home. Several horses were in the stalls, but only one sported white bandages on his forelegs. Killian went straight to it and entered the gelding's roomy stall. Running a hand along his sleek back, Killian walked the length of the horse and back. She stroked his big, blazed face and examined his teeth, gums, ears and eyes.

"He's healthy," Gus said. He stood outside the stall, arms crossed on the top bar, his square chin resting on his checked shirtsleeve. "Other than the marks below his knees."

"May I remove the bandages?"

"Sure. Want me to do it?"

"Yes. He's more comfortable around you. I'm a stranger to him."

"There's no such thing to a Hollywood horse, but I don't mind obliging you." He stepped into the stall, scratched the horse between the ears, then dropped to his haunches to remove the clean bandages.

"Is it bad?" Killian asked, bending at the waist and looking over Gus's shoulder. "The marks, I mean. Are they deep?"

"Deep enough to leave scars, I reckon."

"Do you have a theory as to how they got there?" When Killian moved to one side, rays of sunlight fell upon slashing cuts running horizontally below the horse's knees. Swelling was apparent but the medicine seemed to be reducing it.

"Sure, I got a theory." Gus swiveled on the balls of his feet to look up at her. "Trip-wire, pure and simple. Want to run me in now or wait until tomorrow?"

"Gus, please." She sighed, backing away from him. "Can we work together on this?"

"You want to consort with the enemy?"

"I want to find out who's responsible for that," she said, pointing to the horse's injuries. "Don't you?"

He turned back to the horse. "Every time I look at this, I get sick in my gut. I've worked hard for a clean name in this business and now this..." he said in a trailing voice, shaking his head.

"I talked to a few people about you," she tossed out. "Everyone I spoke with said you were the best in the business and that you'd never trip-wire a horse."

"That's right. I wouldn't." He replaced the bandages with careful hands. The gelding stood perfectly still, not showing either fear or discomfort. "But somebody sure as hell did."

"And we're going to find out who," she said, trying on a friendly smile. "Until this thing is settled there's going to be a spot on your clean reputation, and neither one of us wants that."

"In other words, you're on my side."

"I'm on his side," she corrected, looking at the horse. "And so are you. Right?"

He stood up and ran a hand down the animal's broad face. "Right." Glancing at her, he kept his scowl in place even though she was still smiling. "I guess you'll be wanting to talk to my wranglers."

"Yes, but first I'll talk with Bishop and let him know how I intend to conduct the investigation. It's procedure."

Tipping his head to one side, he looked thoughtful. "And I'm completely off the hook, is that what you're telling me?"

"Well, you weren't here when this took place," she said, and he nodded. "And everyone says you would never harm any of your animals."

"And that's all it takes to prove me innocent?"

"You're already innocent. I'm here to prove guilt." She flinched, hearing how that sounded. "Or, rather, I'm here to find the truth. Somebody's guilty."

"Maybe I told one of my men to go ahead and rig the trip-wire if the director insisted on it," he said, giving her a cagey look that made her squirm inside. "Or maybe I left *knowing* that the director would do something like this and I'd be in the clear because I wouldn't be around. You figure something's going to happen—something you don't like or agree with—so you turn the other cheek, make yourself scarce."

She gave him a long, cool appraisal. "You don't seem as if you're the kind of man who turns the other cheek, Gus."

"Is that your woman's intuition working?"

"I suppose so. I keep thinking of the man I met yesterday—the one who offered me his motel room while he ended up sleeping in a horse trailer. I liked him. I trusted him. He was a perfect gentleman."

One corner of his mouth twitched. "Nobody's perfect."

Seeing she was getting nowhere fast, Killian heaved a sigh of resignation. "Okay. Bottom line. You're not completely off the hook, but you're also not my prime suspect. I think one of your wranglers rigged the wire."

"As soon as you know, I want to know." With jerky, angry actions, he pulled on rawhide gloves.

"So you can fire him?"

He grinned, but it wasn't pleasant. "After."

"After?"

"After I skin him."

TWO DAYS LATER Killian was familiar with the lay of the land. Having interviewed all the wranglers, the director, and his assistants, and having conferred with the animal rights representative assigned to the production, she felt less like an enemy and more like a colleague. The movie wranglers were a friendly bunch, much like the rest of the film crew, and the cast was polite, if aloof. Jerry Bishop was still condescending and ingratiating, but Killian had learned how to deal with him.

All the while, Gus had stayed in the background, discreet but ever-watchful like an old-fashioned chaperon, especially when Killian had interviewed his nephew, Cody, a likable young man with a boyish grin and very little maturity. It was obvious to Killian that Gus was protective toward Cody, although it seemed to her Cody could take care of himself.

Approaching the stables, Killian ducked inside and made her way to her favorite horse, a gentle mare named Rosebud. She pulled a carrot from the pocket of her windbreaker and fed it to the horse, cooing softly as Rosebud nuzzled the palm of her hand and crunched on the carrot.

"What in tarnation do you think you're doing!"

She spun around at the gruff command, but instead of finding a disgruntled bully she realized she'd just been fooled by one of Cody Turnage's endless string of pranks. Aware that she'd placed her hand high over her heart, she released her breath and made a throwaway gesture at the chuckling twenty-two-year-old.

"Very funny. I didn't hear you come in."

"You were too busy cooing and clucking at that horse," he said, looking past her to Rosebud's glistening eyes. "She's a gentle, old soul, isn't she?"

"Yes, do you use her often?" Killian asked, turning back to the mare to stroke her pale gold mane.

"Mostly with kids. There's a ten-year-old boy in this film, but he won't get here until next week. He'll ride her in a couple of scenes."

"I stopped in to check on Gold Dollar," he said. "He's healing up real fast."

"Yes, but he'll be scarred."

"Oh, yeah. Well…" Cody shrugged. "That's a shame, but at least he's not lame." He sauntered to the stall and stroked Gold Dollar's sleek neck. "Hey, partner, how's it going today?"

Killian watched the interaction, smiling to herself at Cody's purring tone of voice. Like his uncle, he seemed to have an affinity for the stock. But, during her interview with him, he'd been so nervous—so wound up that he never once looked in her eye; this was uncharacteristic behavior since, on most occasions, he was an outrageous tease.

"Hey, you going to Billy Ray's tonight?" he asked, spinning around to face her.

She smiled, having heard of Billy Ray's Bar and Grill often since she'd arrived on the set. "Do you go there every night after work?"

"Just about. Sometimes I go to Texas Pete's. That's a honky-tonk on the other side of Bartlesville. It's wild when there's a good band, but they've got a bunch of hillbillies from Branson playing there this week, so I think I'll pass. You going?"

"To Billy Ray's?" Killian clarified, then shook her head. "No, I don't think so."

"Why not?" Cody came toward her, his long, thin legs encased in a pair of jeans that were more suggestive than stylish. "It'll be fun, and the more pretty girls there, the better." He grinned, showing off his straight teeth beneath a sparse, sable-colored mustache, which he undoubtedly thought made him look older. "Come on, hon. I'll be around for you in my pick-me-up at seven. You're in room twelve at the Sunset Motel, aren't you?"

"Yes, that's right." She narrowed her eyes, wondering when he'd found that out and why. "But don't bother. It's out of your way and—"

"No, it's not. I'm picking up Janet Brubaker there, too. She's one of the makeup girls. She's in room sixteen. So you see?" He reached for one of her hands and gave it a squeeze. "It'll work out perfect and you'll have a rip-roarin' time." He winked at her. "I'll see to it, sugar."

"Cody, Cody, Cody," Killian chanted, amused by his blatant flirtation. "You really know how to shovel it, don't you? And here I am without my hip boots on."

He released a hoot of pleasure. "So, you'll be ready at seven?"

"Yes. All right." She made a helpless gesture. "I might as well."

He started backing away, wagging one finger at her. "You'll catch more flies with honey."

"What's that mean?"

"It means that folks might open up if they feel you're one of 'em."

"Then you think someone's been withholding information from me?"

"Naw. I was just slapping my gums. What do I know about it? Nothing." He lost his goofy smile and spun around, his long legs swallowing up acreage as he hurried away. "See ya'!"

Staring after him, Killian wondered if Cody was the one keeping secrets. Did he know something or was he just running off at the mouth, as he'd said? It was hard to tell with someone so young and cocky. Picking up her folder, she flipped through her notes on Cody until she found the name she'd been looking for.

Janet Brubaker, the assistant makeup artist—and Cody's alibi. He'd said he'd been visiting with her when the trip-wire incident supposedly took place, although no one was sure when it had happened. Through painstaking questioning, Killian had targeted the time of the incident to somewhere near the end of the shooting day, at around five-thirty when the sunlight was adequate, but waning. She hadn't questioned Janet extensively, but maybe she should, Killian thought. Janet had confirmed she'd been with Cody, but had been vague about what time it had been or how long Cody had visited her in the makeup trailer that afternoon.

Killian closed her notebook, sensing that, slowly but surely, the finger was pointing at Cody Turnage. The trouble was he wasn't just a wrangler employed by August Breedlove. He was family. Gus's nephew. If her hunches were right, she might as well bury whatever hopes she still had about Gus and her. Chewing fretfully on her lower lip, she hoped she was wrong about Cody. For Gus's sake. And, for her sake.

BILLY RAY'S WAS SO NOISY Killian thought earplugs should have been handed out at the door. As soon as they were inside Cody hooked an arm around Janet's waist and disappeared into the crowd of two-steppers, leaving Killian to fend for herself.

Making her way slowly to the bar, Killian ordered a light beer and then inched toward the back room of the L-shaped honky-tonk where pool tables and pinball machines sat beneath amber-tinted light fixtures. It wasn't so crowded there and voices were kept low in respect for the pool players and pinball wizards. Only a few females were among the colony of stickmen and flipper pressers.

Killian leaned back against the wall and sipped her beer while the music in the other room tried to tempt her back into the mob of dancers. She amused herself by watching the pool games in progress. The center table attracted the most attention. The group surrounding it parted to give the players more elbow and rump room and Killian's interest soared when she recognized the player setting up for a difficult shot. Gus. What was it about him that made her giddy, made her feel warm inside and out? She could barely hear the music over her drumming heartbeats. The man definitely had her number.

Leaning over the table, his belt buckle flush against it, Gus stretched out and took a bead down the length of his pool cue. His back was to Killian, giving her a stunning view of broad shoulders straining against a black, Western-cut shirt. White piping made a loop between his shoulder blades. His jeans and boots were black as well. The only other contrast of color was provided by the silver in his dark hair and his shiny belt buckle. He made the shot and a collective sigh rose in appreciation as he sized up his next attack. Moving around the table with a liquid, agile tread, he measured distances with his eyes and stood at one end of the table for a long view. Now Killian could see his profile, outlined by amber light. His was a strong profile with a straight-bridged, prominent nose, a short, square chin and a broad, smooth forehead. His lashes were long, curling at the tips.

He cocked a hip, splayed his hand on the green-topped table, propped the stick on it and followed through with one fluid motion. The ball rolled and smacked into another, which in turn, cannoned into a side pocket. The game was won.

Victorious, he accepted the round of handshakes and congratulations he was offered, then shook his head when someone challenged him to another game. It was then, as he strode toward the archway leading to the other part of the bar, that he saw her. His stride shortened a fraction, then he continued on with grim determination. He would have walked right past her if she hadn't reached out and hooked her fingers in the crook of his arm.

"You can't even say hello?" Killian demanded, her anger sparked by his intentional slight.

"Hello." His glance was stinging, arctic. "I was going in there for a beer."

"Here. Have mine." She shoved the cold mug into his hand. "I've taken a couple of sips, but I promise you won't catch anything from me except, maybe, some good manners, which certainly won't hurt you."

His stare warmed a few degrees, then he brought the mug to his lips and drank the beer in several long swallows. He returned the empty mug to her and his lips twisted into something that was neither a smile, nor a smirk.

"There, and thanks. I was dry."

"So I see." She stared at the foam left on the sides of the glass. "I haven't seen anyone chugalug a beer like that since I was in college."

"When was that? Last week?"

"You silver-tongued devil," she teased, and won an honest-to-goodness smile from him. "I'm thirty." She arched one eyebrow, but as he wouldn't reveal his age, she made an impatient gesture. "Come on, come on. I told you, now you have to tell me. How old are you?"

"Thirty-four but I've got a lot of miles on me."

"Why were you snubbing me?"

"When?"

She pulled an exaggerated frown. "Just now. You were going to walk right past me."

"Oh." He shrugged, dismissing his bad manners. "It was for your benefit. I didn't think you'd want to fraternize with the guy you're investigating."

"I'm investigating an incident, not you," she reminded him.

Some people squeezed behind him, trying to fit into the archway, and he leaned into Killian, flattening her against the wall. He raised one arm, propping the heel of his hand above Killian's head. His nearness shortened her breath and clutched her heart. She could do nothing but look up into his eyes and silently will him to thaw. He did, little by little, his head moving down, down, down until his mouth hovered a bare inch from hers.

Could someone die from anticipation? she wondered, slipping her hand up his chest and around to the back of his neck. His hair was silk against her fingers.

"Do you dance?"

"Dance? On occasion."

"How about it?"

"You want to *dance?*"

"Sure." He bobbed one shoulder. "Why not? Just don't expect much. My Arthur Murray days are far behind me."

"Don't worry. My expectations just plummeted."

He grasped her hand and pulled her along behind him as he wound through the crowd to the packed dance floor. A snappy chart-buster blared from the jukebox. Just as they found an empty spot and faced each other, the song ended. With one hand still held by his, Killian waited for the next number to start. The opening bars revealed a slow ballad, sung by a popular songstress whose voice could make even the toughest heart ache a little. One corner of Gus's mouth inched up as he took Killian in his arms and began moving with her to the music. She traced the trimming across the back of his shirt and tried to identify his cologne. Gradually, she relaxed and began to enjoy her consolation prize. Dancing was better than nothing, she told herself. Better than being enemies, but not better than a kiss would have been. She looked up into his eyes and discovered a slumberous sensuality in them that stirred something inside her.

"I guess it's true about music soothing the savage beast," she said, smiling. "A few minutes ago I wouldn't have believed we could be enjoying each other's company. In fact, I got the distinct impression earlier that you were bound and determined to brush me off."

"It's hard to keep your distance on a dance floor," he explained. "But we should be careful."

"Careful of what?" she asked, pulling way from him.

He sighed, irritated. "You're investigating me, remember?"

"So? There's no reason why we can't be friendly."

"I don't want anyone to think I'm trying to get on your good side so you'll exonerate me." He glanced around nervously at the other dancers and smiled.

"Do you really believe that one dance with you could be construed as some kind of bribe?" Killian asked, hoping he was kidding.

"Stranger things have happened."

She jerked away from him, incensed. "It would take a lot more than that for me to jeopardize my job." She backed farther out of his reach, glaring at him. "You know, you're not the only one with a reputation to protect, Breedlove." Not giving him a chance to retort, she turned on her heel and wove through the couples. Reaching the door, she pushed past a couple of new arrivals and stumbled outside.

The night air felt cool and pure on her overheated skin. She brushed angry tears from the corners of her eyes and called herself every kind of fool for letting him get to her. The door opened behind her and she glanced back, groaning when she saw Gus.

"Please, just go back inside," she said, fishing her car keys from her purse and then realizing her car was parked at the motel. "Oh, damn."

"Need a ride?"

"Not from you."

He stepped neatly in front of her, blocking her escape route. "It's a long walk back to the motel."

"You're not the only man here with a car, Breedlove."

"I liked it better when you called me Gus."

Giving up any hope of putting him off, she locked gazes with him. "Is this your pitiful attempt at an apology?"

His eyes glimmered in the moonlight. "No," he said in a voice suddenly rough and raspy. "This is." And then his arms were around her and his mouth was warming hers.

Killian stiffened, then grew pliant in his embrace. His kiss dissolved into a series of lipping bites, each one touching off sparks. She held his head between her hands and drank him in as if he were a lover's potion. Just when she thought her knees would give out, he set her from him.

"Now, can I drive you back to your motel?" he asked, his voice still husky with passion. "All's forgiven?"

Killian smiled, shaking her head to clear it. "You wish. Do you think a few kisses makes everything better?" She stopped smiling. "No way, cowboy. I've bent over backward trying to gain your friendship, your trust, but after tonight I can see that's impossible." She started for his pickup, her feelings in a turmoil.

"Killian," he said, his voice carrying easily. "Nothing's impossible."

3

TRYING HER BEST to appear nonchalant, Killian twisted sideways and stared out the window of the pickup truck. Even though there was nothing to see—except total darkness—she couldn't look at Gus. Being close to him was unnerving enough. He was whistling a happy tune beside her and that only added to her discomfort.

She was angry, but she was also attracted to him. In the confines of the pickup she could smell his after-shave and something else—him. Masculine. Earthy. Masterfully sensuous.

When he brought the pickup to a smooth stop in front of her motel, she would have catapulted out the door if he hadn't clamped one hand on her arm. The contact sent a quivering awareness through her. Did he feel it, too? She wondered if she was the only one who responded to every touch, every smile, every word. It made it damned hard to stay mad at him. She had to keep reminding herself that he'd acted like a jackass back at Billy Ray's.

"Not so fast," he said, wagging a finger at her. "A gentleman walks a lady to her door."

She looked blankly at him. "What has that got to do with you?"

"Funny." Nothing in his expression confirmed that statement. In fact, he looked aggravated. He rolled out of the truck seat and hit the ground with long, leggy strides.

She thought of opening the door and vaulting from the truck before he could stride around to her side but her good sense prevailed. *Don't make a federal case out of it,* she cautioned herself. *In a few minutes he'll be gone and this ordeal will be history.*

He flung back the door and offered her his hand. Her fingers barely touched his as she stepped out and then she hurried across the parking lot to her room. He was right on her heels. She unlocked the door, stumbled inside and then whirled to give him the bum's rush.

"I'm in, safe and sound, and you're now free to leave. Good night." She started to close the door in his face but his boot prevented that, then his shoulder widened the space until Killian had no choice but to hear him out.

"I guess I've got a chip on my shoulder," he said with a shrug.

Killian laughed harshly. "Chip? I hate to tell you, but from here it looks like you're a hunchback."

"Can you blame me?"

"Yes." She tapped one foot and crossed her arms, adopting the age-old posture of a woman scorned.

"Okay." He tucked the tips of his fingers into the front pockets of his jeans and tried to look sheepish. "Please accept my apology for coming on a little too strong back there."

"A little too strong?"

"Are you going to throw my words back in my face all night?"

She inched the door shut, hoping he'd retreat. "I'm not going to do *anything* with you all night."

"Killian," he said, a touch of exasperation in his tone. "How are we going to work together if you won't forgive me for being a chump?"

"Work together?" She laughed when he glowered at her repetition. "Sorry. Okay, okay. I forgive you. Are you serious about working together? My investigation will go a lot faster if you cooperate instead of treating me like your mortal enemy."

"I don't usually kiss my mortal enemies."

Feeling her face flame, she averted her gaze. When he stepped forward, she was already off balance and he was inside her room before she knew it.

"I don't remember inviting you in," she objected weakly.

"Got any leads yet?" he asked, closing the door and lounging back against it.

"I've interviewed the key people . . ."

"And?"

She hedged, wondering how to drop the next bomb. "And the only one so far acting the least bit strange is Cody." She winced as his gaze sharpened. "He seems real nervous...kind of evasive about where he was and what he was doing that afternoon."

"Cody wouldn't hurt the livestock." His tone was almost threatening.

Killian shrugged. "I've got a lot more ground to cover before I can zero in on anybody."

"Cody's just a kid. Anybody would be nervous having you sniffing around and—" He turned his head as noises floated in from outside. A squeal pierced the air and he opened the door and stepped outside to investigate.

Killian followed him, drawn by the giggles and shrieks of delight. Clearly three sheets to the wind, Cody Turnage was chasing Janet Brubaker around his truck. Janet slowed down enough for him to catch her, then squealed when he picked her up in his arms and carried her toward her motel room.

"Hey there, Uncle Gus!" Cody called, grinning like a chimp. "I see you hooked up with a female, too. Have a good 'un." He sent them a lascivious wink.

"We're not... I'm not..." Killian ceased her babbling, realizing that Cody wasn't listening. "I'll have to straighten him out when he's not pickled."

"He won't even remember this tomorrow morning, so don't worry about it." Gus chuckled and ran a hand over his mouth. "How can you think a fun-lovin' kid like Cody could be cruel to anything or anybody?"

"Sometimes people act against their better judgment if the price is right."

"You think he took a bribe?" Gus asked, rounding on her.

"I think that whoever trip-wired that horse didn't do it for the heck of it. They either got money for it or their job was threatened had they refused."

"So you think I might have ordered him to trip-wire the horse or I'd fire him?"

"Will you quit getting all huffy every time we discuss this?" She heaved a sigh. "All I'm doing is throwing out possibilities."

"Sounds like you're accusing my nephew and I don't like it one little bit."

"Is this how we're going to work together? Look, if I knew what happened, I would have filed my official report by now. I wish we could talk about this without you getting all riled up." She went back inside. When she turned to tell Gus good-night, he was already climbing behind the wheel of his truck. He didn't even wave goodbye.

She was about to close her door when Cody and Janet set up another racket. Cody stumbled out of Janet's room, hat and boots in hand.

"Aww, baby, I didn't mean nothing by that. Let me come back inside and make it up to you."

"No. How dare you call me by some other girl's name! Who is Christy anyway?"

Killian inched her door closed, but left just enough space to eavesdrop.

"I don't know, doll-baby. I was just talking. I swear I don't know any girl by that name."

"Liar," Janet screamed, shaking one fist at Cody. "You'd better be good to me or I'll tell the truth about you, Cody Wayne Turnage."

Cody lunged forward, one hand batting the air in a shushing motion. "Watch your mouth! She's liable to hear you."

Killian shut the door all the way and hoped Cody hadn't seen that it had been ajar. A few minutes later she heard tires churn gravel into dust and she looked out the window to see the red taillights of Cody's truck.

Before she went to bed she added some notes to Cody Turnage's file.

CODY WAS POLISHING the silver disks on his saddle when Killian found him in the stables. When he saw her she noticed how he looked away quickly as if he didn't want to meet her eyes.

"Hi, Cody," she said, standing beside him. "My, my. That's a pretty saddle."

"Yeah. I bought it off one of the other guys. He had it made special in Taos last year. This is all hand-tooled and there's not another like it in the whole world. I never thought the guy would sell it. Guess I made him the right offer."

Killian ran one fingertip over the fragile apple blossoms cut into the suede. "Cost you a lot of money, I imagine."

Cody stiffened and covered the saddle with a large chamois. "Not so much," he mumbled, then made an attempt at changing the subject. "Hey there, pretty thing. You ran out on us last night." He scratched at the day-old stubble on his chin. "Seems to me I recall something about you and Uncle Gus getting it on. I'm glad you're keeping it in the family." He wiggled his eyebrows and grinned. "Did the earth move, darlin'? The ladies say Uncle Gus is a stallion between the sheets."

She knew what he was up to and wasn't about to let him get the upper hand. Flipping back one corner of the chamois, she ran her other hand over the silver-capped saddle horn. "How much did this set you back, Cody?"

Ruddy color stained his cheeks. "Not much. It was a steal."

"How much?"

"A few hundred is all."

"You're doing all right for a junior wrangler."

"I'm more than that," he objected hotly. "I went to wrangler classes *and* stunt school."

"Yes, but you've only worked on two films before this one and Gus has gotten you every single job."

"So? We're family. Nothing wrong with family helping family."

"How did you get enough money to afford this saddle?" she repeated.

Cody ran his tongue along the inside of his cheek and stared at her for a few long moments before he answered, "I saved it."

"You don't strike me as the frugal type." She knew she couldn't risk giving him any slack or she'd find herself talking to thin air.

He covered the saddle again with the chamois. Muscles twitched along his jawline and the color drained from his face. He looked achingly young and definitely scared. "Are you accusing me of taking money to trip that horse?"

"I'm just wondering where you got the money to buy this saddle."

Sweat broke out across his forehead. "That's none of your business." He shouldered past her. "I thought we were friends, but I can see now that you're out to finger me for something I had nothing to do with. If you don't back off, I'm going to tell my uncle."

"Go ahead and tell him," Killian shouted at his back.

"He sure won't be sharing the sheets with you again if I do," Cody retorted over his shoulder.

"We're not— Cody!" she called after him but he kept walking until he was out of sight. Killian kicked the nearest stall door and hoped to high heaven that Cody wasn't spreading gossip about her and Gus. He was certainly immature enough to do such a thing. That's all she needed, she thought with a groan. Nothing like being the object of gossip over something she hadn't even done— yet.

Yet...She smiled ruefully. The chances of her and Gus getting involved were growing fainter and fainter as her suspicions about his nephew grew stronger and stronger. Killian examined the saddle again. It was the kind of outfit few cowboys could afford. Her intuition told her she was on the right trail.

Outside the stables she rounded a corner and bounced off a solid chest. Gus. He helped her regain her balance by placing his large hands on her shoulders.

"Hot on somebody's trail?" he asked, grinning.

A wave of guilt pounded her. She wiggled from his grasp and brushed wrinkles from the sleeves of her plaid shirt. Anything to avoid his eyes.

"Will I see you tonight?" he asked.

"Tonight? Am I supposed to be somewhere tonight?"

"Cast and crew are invited to a barbecue restaurant in town."

"I'm not cast or crew."

"But I am, and I'm inviting you."

"Why?"

He threw his head back as if she'd taken a swipe at him. "Why not? You don't think I'm trying to sweeten your pot, do you? If that was my motive, I'd be taking you to my trailer instead of to a barbecue pit."

His phrasing amused her and she relaxed. "You live in a trailer? Not a horse trailer, I hope."

"No, a travel one. It's out behind the makeup trailers. The white one with blue and gray stripes, if you're wondering."

"I wasn't," she fibbed. He had an uncanny ability to read her mind. Giving him a once-over, she saw that he was in a much better mood than he had been last night. In fact, he was more like the man she'd met on that rainy night—friendly, sexy, interested in her as a potential lover instead of a potential enemy. "So you're going to the restaurant tonight for dinner?"

"I am if you are."

"What if I'm not," she teased.

"What have you got in mind?"

She hesitated, wondering if she dared speak her mind. His smile helped her find the courage. His smile was boyish, giving him a look of everlasting youthfulness. "I'd like to get far, far away from the madding crowd. A little peace and quiet is more my speed, but I can understand you wanting to be with your buddies."

"Did I say anything about wanting to be with buddies?" He thumbed back the brim of his Stetson so that the sun could hit him full in the face. He squinted, his eyes becoming dark, thickly lashed slits. "I want to be with you."

"Why?" she asked, too quickly and too sharply. "I mean, after last night I wouldn't think that you—"

"I don't remember last night," he interrupted. "How about coming around to my place around eight for hamburgers?"

"I don't want you to cook when you were planning to eat out."

"Cook? Hell, that's not cooking. All I'll do is throw some meat on the grill." He looked past her and raised a hand in answer to a summons. "I've got to run. You'll be on my doorstep around eight, right?"

Killian glanced over her shoulder at the two wranglers waiting patiently for their boss to join them. "Yes. I'll be there."

"You bring dessert," he said, striding past.

"Wh-what?" she asked. "Dessert? What should I—I don't know what to bring and I don't have a way to—"

Turning, he walked backward. He shook a finger at her and squinted one eye cagily. "Either bring dessert or *be* dessert, darlin'. It's the law in these parts."

"JANET!" Tucking the store-bought tray of brownies under one arm, Killian gestured to Janet Brubaker with the other. The brunette had just locked the door of the makeup trailer and she waved back at Killian.

"Hi. Need a ride to the restaurant? You're going to eat barbecue with the rest of us, aren't you?"

"Uh, no. I—I, uh, made other plans," Killian said. "Do you have a minute? I need to talk to you." Sensing Janet's reluctance, Killian ran up the steps of the trailer and pinned Janet on the small porch, blocking her exit. "I'll make it fast. I know you're anxious to join the others."

Janet sighed with extreme boredom, eyeing Killian as if she were Bad Luck personified. "You're going to pass up barbecued pig for those grocery store brownies? Girl, you need to have your taste buds tuned. They've gone flat."

"No, this is dessert." She examined the sweets. When she'd put them under her arm, she'd smashed them and they hardly looked like something one would want to put in one's mouth. "They're my substitute."

"For what?"

"Never mind." She held the brownies behind her back. "Janet, are you sure Cody was with you the afternoon the horse was hurt?"

"I said he was, didn't I?"

"Yes, but I want you to be certain." Killian locked gazes with her. "It's important, Janet. That poor horse can't point the finger at the person who wounded him. It's up to all of us to find that person and make sure he or she is punished."

"Gold Dollar's going to be okay."

"Yes, but he's scarred for life. Gus won't use him again because his trust has been broken. He'll be too flighty in stunts after this. Don't you see, Janet? We can't allow even one animal to be harmed on a movie set or people will think they can take advantage of them." She took a deep breath and cautioned herself against sermonizing. "What time did Cody arrive here that afternoon, Janet?"

"I told you."

"Tell me again."

"Three or four."

"Which was it, three or four?"

"I don't know. Three, I guess."

"He knocked off work that early?"

"No, work wasn't over. I was busy right up to six."

"But Cody wasn't, right? He hung around in this trailer all that time, cooling his heels and waiting for you to get off work? Why wasn't he working? Was he goofing off because his uncle was out of town?"

"No," Janet said hotly. "He worked even harder while Gus was away."

"Then why was he sitting around on his lazy butt for three hours?" Killian asked, being purposefully provocative.

"He wasn't!"

Killian leaned one hip against the banister. "Do tell, and this time tell the truth."

Janet drew in a ragged breath. "Look, all I know is that Cody came to the trailer around three. I wasn't watching him every minute. I was busy, okay? When I finished work, he was still here."

"But he could have ducked out for an hour or so and you wouldn't have noticed. Is that what you're telling me?"

"He could have, but I don't know that he did. He says he didn't." Janet glanced at her watch, squinting to make out the time in the gathering dusk. "It's almost eight and I'm all talked out where you're concerned." She planted a hand against Killian's shoulder and shoved her to one side. "S'cuse me." Janet squirmed past Killian and darted to her pink Mustang convertible.

Killian watched her hasty getaway and assimilated the information. As far as she was concerned, Cody's alibi had just been blown sky-high. She descended the steps slowly, lost in thought, then blinked aside her musings and remembered that Janet had said it was almost eight.

"The witching hour," she murmured. "Or is it the warlock hour?" Looking in the general direction of Gus's trailer, she wondered if he was flying around his place in nervous anticipation of her visit.

Leaving her car where she'd parked it beside the makeup and hairstylists' trailers, she headed for Gus's place, swinging her purse in one hand and the dessert in the—

"Oh, shoot!" Killian stared at the massacred brownies. They were worse off than they had been before. She remembered having leaned against the railing. "Guess I leaned against these, too." She tried to poke them into squares again through the wrinkled plastic, but no matter what she tried, she couldn't make them look appetizing. "They'll have to do. I'm sure not going into the lion's den empty-handed."

Approaching his trailer, she was drawn by the aroma of smoked meat. A charcoal cooker sat in front of Gus's trailer. He stood in front of it, his back to Killian. Spatula in hand, he lifted the cooker's lid and a cloud of aromatic smoke rose and encircled him.

"Make mine medium rare," Killian called out.

Gus spun around. He wore a chef's apron with Kiss the Cook printed on it. Killian was sorely tempted.

"Is that dessert?" Gus asked. "How disappointing. I was hoping you'd be the dessert."

"Not on your life." She handed him the remains and grimaced at his wide-eyed reaction. "I'm sure they'll *taste* great."

He examined the parcel. "You brought a square of fertilizer?"

"They're brownies," she said, laughing. "I sort of accidentally squashed them. The checker at the grocery store said they're pretty good eating."

"I'm sure they are, if you haven't eaten in a week or two."

"Okay, okay," she surrendered, snatching the brownies from him and tossing them onto the picnic table. "You said bring dessert. You didn't say anything about it having to be pretty." She sniffed the air. "Smells great. I love charcoaled burgers."

"And I love squashed brownies."

"Stop with the brownies already!" She popped him in the shoulder with her fist. "Mind if I go inside to the little girl's room?"

"Be my guest. It's at the back, right off the bedroom."

"Thanks."

"Don't lie down on my bed while you're in there," he called after her, wickedness blazing in his eyes.

"Don't worry, I won't," she assured him, then wished he hadn't planted that tantalizing notion in her head, especially when she'd finished in the bathroom and found herself staring at Gus's island bed. The patchwork coverlet seemed to invite her to sit down and stay awhile, so she did.

Killian bounced on the firm mattress and ran her hands over the handcrafted quilt. She imagined Gus stretched out on it. *Bet he's downright gorgeous in the morning with his hair mussed and his eyes all sleepy*, she thought, then jumped up when she heard his approaching footsteps.

"Ready to eat, Killian?"

"R-ready!" She bustled out of the bedroom and tried not to look guilty. "Can I help you set the table or anything?"

"Table's set." He stood aside, indicating the open front door. "We're dining outside if that's all right with you."

"Fine with me." She went past him, heading for the door.

"Do you think my bed's comfortable?"

"Uh . . . I . . ." She laughed, not knowing what to say. "Lemonade!"

"I never saw a woman get so excited about lemonade," he observed dryly. "Your cheeks are rosy and your eyes are shining like jewels. It's the lemonade that made you breathless, right?"

She pretended to be oblivious to his sarcasm. "It's a beautiful night."

"Sure is." He sat opposite her and handed her a bag of chips. "So, was my bed comfy?"

Glaring at him, she wished she wasn't such a lady and could slap the smirk off his face. "Yes, it's comfortable. Satisfied? Can we talk about something else now? You're the most irritating man I've ever met, August Breed-love. You knew I'd sit on your blasted bed once you put the idea into my head."

"Human nature," he said, winking. "If you study it, life isn't so mysterious."

"I like a little mystery," she said, squirting mustard onto her hamburger bun.

"So do I. Take you, for instance . . ."

"Me? You find me mysterious?"

"Sure do." He put ketchup on his bun and added a few slices of dill pickle. "It's a mystery to me why a beautiful, intelligent woman like you is still running around single."

"It's by choice." She bit into the hamburger and savored the deliciously smoked ground beef.

"Are you against marriage?"

"No, I've been busy." She wrinkled her nose at his burst of laughter. "I *have* been," she asserted. "What about you? How come you're not breeding Breed-loves?"

He smiled at her play on words. "I'm better alone."

She probed him with her eyes, seeking the truth. "You like being alone?"

"I don't always like it, but . . ." He shrugged his broad shoulders. "My life has been—women don't find it attractive. When I'm home, I'm reclusive and when I'm working, I have to travel and stay away for weeks at a time."

"I don't doubt any of that, but I think there are women who'd love that kind of life."

"Would you?"

She swallowed hard, feeling penned in. "Like I said, I keep busy."

"What's that got to do with my question?"

"Well, I'm not the kind of woman who needs a man to . . . you know, make her happy. I'm reclusive, too. I don't mind being alone. I don't think I'd want to be joined at the hip to a man. I need my own space sometimes or I get claustrophobic." She studied his slow grin. "Why are you smiling? Do I sound like I'm ready for a padded room?"

"No. You sound like me, that's all." He dabbed at the corners of his wide mouth with a paper napkin. "When you're raised to be independent, it's tough to all of a sudden be part of a twosome."

Killian nodded, understanding. "But I don't necessarily want to go it alone forever."

His gaze lifted to hers and held on for a few shattering moments. "Neither do I." He sounded puzzled, perplexed, as if his own answer spawned other questions within him.

"When did you decide we were going to be friends, after all?" she asked.

"When I decided you were worth the trouble."

"And what prompted that decision?"

"When I imagined how pretty you'd look on that patchwork quilt in there."

Heat and color swept into her cheeks and her laughter bordered on a nervous twitter. "You say the most outrageous things," she said, deciding to make light of his suggestion.

"You think that's outrageous, do you?"

"I sure do."

"You ain't heard nothin' yet." Popping the last bite of burger into his mouth, he then reached for the smashed brownies and tore off the plastic wrap. "Let's see if that grocery clerk told the truth or sold you a bill of goods." He glanced around. "Thought I had a knife out here, but I guess I'll have to go inside and—"

"Don't bother." She tore off a corner of the damaged goods and placed it on her tongue. The brownies were chewy and rich with chocolate. "Mmm." She nodded. "Not bad. They've even got pecans." Tearing off another chunk, she offered it to him.

Instead of taking it in his hand, he lifted his rump off the bench and leaned over the table to let her place the morsel into his mouth. She pushed the gooey brownie in, but before she could extract her thumb and forefinger, his lips closed on them. Killian jerked her hand back, feeling as if she'd been hit by a bolt of electricity.

Gus smiled and chewed on the brownie.

"They...they're good, huh?" Killian asked, wiping her hands on a napkin then pinching off another bite. It was meant for her, but Gus leaned close again and opened his mouth. She fed it to him quickly, withdrawing her fingers before his lips could capture them.

He caught her wrist and slowly, tauntingly, deliciously, licked the crumbs from her fingers. His brown eyes flirted with her, implying suggestive things that made her blush hotly.

Taking one last lick across the pad of her thumb, he then pressed a moist kiss into her palm. "Looks like you're dessert after all, darlin'."

4

"Is THAT WHY you invited me here?" Killian asked, removing her hand from his. "Just to take advantage of me?"

"No, I invited you here hoping *you'd* take advantage of *me*." He spread out his arms in a gesture of blatant surrender. "All I ask is that you be gentle and that you still respect me in the morning."

She shook a finger at him and rose from the bench. "You're a dangerous man, August Breedlove." Gathering the paper plates, she recognized the fluttering in her stomach and knew Gus had put it there. "I'll help you clean up and then I'd better go."

"Go?" he asked, scoffing at the idea. "Not before we go for a ride. It's a pretty night and we ought to enjoy some of it on horseback, don't you think?"

The suggestion appealed to her. Riding with him was something she'd thought about before. "Sure. I'd love to go riding."

"Great." He stood up and stretched his arms high over his head, giving her a few moments to admire the length and breadth of him. He wore jeans and a blue striped shirt and navy blue vest left unbuttoned. The jeans looked new, probably the pair he saved for special social engagements. "Let's go. I'll saddle Livewire for you."

He locked the front door of the trailer and stuck the keys into his front pocket.

"I was thinking more along the lines of Rosebud," she said, letting him take her hand.

"Old Rosebud wouldn't be able to keep up with Apache. Besides, you need a mount with more spirit."

"Livewire's the pinto mare?"

"That's right. She's got loads of personality. I use her for flashy scenes—bank robberies or train holdups. She's a cutup—pawing the ground and tossing her head. That sort of thing."

"What was Gold Dollar's specialty?"

His mouth turned down at the corners. "Falls. Gold Dollar is a trusting soul—used to be anyway." He glanced around as they made their way toward the stables. "Where's your car?"

"I parked it over by the honey wagons," she said, using the film euphemism for the hair and makeup departments. "I saw Janet and I wanted to talk to her."

"Janet Brubaker," he said, then tilted his head to peer inquiringly at her. "Was she embarrassed about last night?"

"What about last night?" For a moment, Killian had forgotten about the playful scene between Janet and Cody before it had gone sour. "Oh, yes. Right after you left, Janet threw Cody out."

"She did? What for?"

"From what I gathered, he called her by another woman's name."

Gus laughed under his breath. "Some day that boy's going to cross the wrong woman's path and end up with his legs tied in a knot."

"I'm sure he'll sweet-talk his way back into her good graces."

They reached the stables and Gus saddled Livewire, then outfitted Apache, his favorite mount. Killian followed his lead as he set off south toward a wooded area along the creek. The night was pewter gray, lit by stars and a slice of yellow moon. Sitting tall in the saddle, Killian felt at home as she always did on horseback. She'd ridden her first horse by the time she was three and had been bucked off one when she was six. Horses had been a more integral part of her life than automobiles. Breathing in the cool night air, she relaxed, only then realizing how keyed up she'd been. Being with Gus made her wary. It wasn't him that she didn't trust; it was herself. And since the attraction was mutual, that made it all the more dangerous. Glancing sideways at him, she felt her heartbeat accelerate when she found he was looking at her with his usual intensity.

"How did you get involved in the film business?" Killian asked, trying for something safe . . . something that would decrease the ardor in his glittering eyes.

He smiled as if he were on to her game and then trained his gaze straight ahead to the bubbling creek. "A movie company asked to use my property and the pay was right, so I let them set up camp. They stayed six weeks, and by the time they'd left I had decided there was money to be made in the movie business. I went to California and enrolled in stunt school and hooked up with the wrangler association. I left my card all over the place, offering my livestock for films."

"By the time you returned to Oklahoma you had all kinds of offers?" Killian asked, jumping ahead with his story.

"Nothing happened for almost a year and then a company called about a commercial. They needed a herd of cattle for the shoot and I told them to come on down."

"You've got cattle, too?"

"Nope, but I know people who do. I borrowed a herd from a neighbor and paid him a percentage of the fee I was paid. Slowly, a little bit at a time, my name started making the rounds and business picked up. I even started getting some stunt work."

"Now you're one of the top wranglers in the business. You must be proud of that."

"I am...I was." He winced and shook his head. Moonlight played over his inky hair. "Right now my name is mud." He scowled at the red-colored mud along the creek bank and edged his horse away from it.

"We'll clean up your name."

"Sure of that?" he asked, glancing at her sharply.

"Of course."

"If you find out who did it—"

"I will, believe me."

"That still doesn't mean my name will be cleared," he pointed out. "Some people might think I still had something to do with it and I let someone else take the fall."

"Gus, I told you that everyone I talked with swore up and down that you'd never have anything to do with illegal stunts," she reminded him, reining in Livewire.

"Look, let's not talk about this. I'd like to get away from my work tonight." She looked in the opposite direction of the creek. "See that twin-trunked oak up ahead? I'll race you."

"You're on," he said, already whipping Apache around in that direction.

"Go!" Killian pressed her heels into the mare's flanks and the animal leaped into an all-out run. The head start was just enough and she reached the appointed tree a second or two before Gus. Laughing, she swung out of the saddle. "That was fun. There's nothing like a fast horse on flat ground."

"Almost nothing," he agreed, throwing one leg over and sliding to the ground. He came straight for her and his arms were around her before she could manage a protest. "I can think of only one thing more thrilling."

"Gus, you idiot, let me—"

He rubbed a soft kiss against her lips. The promise of more to come took her breath away. She wound her arms around his neck and kissed him as if there were no tomorrow because for them that might be true. Tomorrow might make them enemies. The situation was that explosive and they both knew it. When his tongue touched hers it seemed that the bottom dropped out of the earth. She fell to her knees and then she was lying on the ground with him, lying in the tall, whispering grass, wrapped in his arms and loving every moment of it.

He wanted her and he made no attempt to hide it. He pulled her shirt from her jeans and his hands moved up under it to stroke her back and waist. Killian made a helpless sound, wanting him, too, but finding it difficult to let herself go completely. Reality kept tapping her on the shoulder and reminding her of the consequences of mindless desire.

His lips created sparks down the side of her neck. He nipped her shoulder, taking a gentle love bite, and she laughed. It would be so lovely to be loved by him, she thought. To be rocked in his arms, cradled in his capable hands.

As he inched her blouse higher and higher to expose her breasts, she told herself to stop him while she had the strength of will to do it, but he was the one to suddenly sit up and edge away from her. He ran a hand through his dusky hair and released his breath in a choppy sigh.

"We can't do this," he said, his voice unraveling.

"Wh-what?" Killian straightened her blouse and pushed her hair away from her face. "What's wrong?"

"We can't do this, Killian," he said, looking around at her. "I want to make love to you but it's not right—not while you're investigating me and zeroing in on my nephew. If you'd only see it my way. . ."

"What do you mean?" She rose to her knees to shove her shirttails back inside her jeans.

"Nothing. Forget it. I just hope your investigation has a happy ending, Killian."

"But what if it doesn't?" She wanted him to tell her that it wouldn't matter but she knew he wouldn't lie. "Will you still want me as much as you do right now?"

He opened his mouth, then shut it and looked away from her probing eyes. "I don't know. I'm not sure." His gaze returned to hers, rock-steady. "Maybe we should be getting back."

"Yes, let's." She gathered the reins and pulled herself up into the saddle again.

"You don't think Janet had anything to do with the trip-wire, do you?"

"Do you?" she asked, wondering what was on his mind.

"I don't see how she could have. Why were you talking to her?"

"She's Cody's alibi." She hated the way he looked at her—as if she were a traitor. "Look, Gus, I'm just doing my job."

"Cody didn't do it. Ask anybody."

"That's what I'm doing. I'm asking everybody."

"And?" he asked, his voice as sharp as a whip.

"And I'll let you know when I get something solid." She sent him a gentle smile and hoped he'd take her next words kindly. "I'm afraid you're setting yourself up for a big fall."

"And I'm afraid you're barking up the wrong tree." His chin jutted out, stubborn and defiant. "Cody's young and impulsive. He's a charmer and a ladies' man, but he'd never hurt any of our livestock. I raised him better than that."

"*You* raised him? Where's his father?"

"His father was a serviceman who died when Cody was a toddler. I'm like a father to him. He wouldn't double-cross me."

"He might not have seen it that way. You know...what you don't know, can't hurt you. Maybe that's how Cody justified it."

His eyes snapped warnings. "I want you to lay off that kid."

"No." She tipped up her chin, matching her stubborn streak to his. "He's a suspect and this is my investigation."

He laughed without humor. "Right, it's *your* investigation and *my* reputation hangs in the balance."

"Gus..." She reached out to him, but he kneed Apache and galloped away from her. She stared after him, dismay wilting her spirits. The man was too stubborn and too gorgeous for his own good, she thought, then she smiled grimly. He was probably thinking the same thing about her.

IT HAD BEEN one of those days. Hell on wheels.

Slamming the door behind her to let off a little steam, Killian tossed her briefcase and purse onto the motel bed and kicked off her pinching shoes. She started morosely at the inch-wide run snaking up her nylon and groaned as she stomped into the bathroom. She braced her hands on either side of the washbasin and stared at herself in the mirror above it. An angry, young woman looked back at her—blond hair tumbling over her forehead, blue eyes smoldering with fury. Pressure built behind those eyes and she wasn't sure if she was on the brink of a headache or a crying jag.

"Ooo, I hate Jerry Bishop," she said between clenched teeth, recalling the director's smugness when she'd questioned him. "I know he knows something, that weasel, and I'm going to find out if it's the last thing I do!"

Her loud voice bounced off the tile walls and she forced herself to take a few deep breaths while she counted to ten . . . then counted to ten again. Snatches of her earlier conversation with the director circled in her mind like dust devils. He'd almost challenged her to finger him, the creep!

"If you can pin it on me, go for it, honey," Killian said, repeating what Jerry Bishop had told her, word for word. "But heed this warning before you take out after me. I'll phrase it in a way a country girl like you can understand—if you can't run fast enough to keep up with the big dogs, then you'd better stay on the porch." She ended her recitation with an imitation of the smirk he'd extended her. "Well, get ready, Mr. Bishop," she said in a low, growling voice. "This dog is going to be nipping at your butt from here on in."

She rummaged through her toiletries until she found the bottle of aspirin. Prying open the lid, she tapped the bottle for two tablets. A loud rapping sounded on her motel door and she jerked, sending aspirin flying like pellets from a shotgun.

"Damnation!" she yelled, her aggravation overflowing. She charged from the bathroom with blood in her eyes and threw the door open wide. "What now?" she asked, glaring at Gus. "Go ahead, take your best shot."

He stumbled back. "Why are you acting like a mad dog?"

"Why is everyone comparing me to canines?" she demanded, then stepped back and motioned annoyingly for him to enter. He did, but she noticed he kept his distance. "So what brings you here, Gus? Have you got more orders for me about how you want me to run my investigation?"

"You're in a rotten mood, huh?"

She smiled sourly. "How did you guess?" She raised the leg with the racing stripe. "See this? I got that on a file cabinet in Jerry Bishop's office. He was giving me the bum's rush and I wasn't taking too kindly to it. This is my reward for trying to be civil to that baboon. But don't you worry," she said, lifting a finger and narrowing her eyes wickedly, "because he hasn't heard the last of me yet. I have more nylons and more questions."

"I'm relieved to hear you're badgering somebody else other than my nephew."

"I suppose that's why you're here," she said, crossing her arms and waiting for the inevitable.

"You questioned him about his saddle. He told me you all but accused him of taking money to trip-wire that horse so he could buy it."

"If you weren't related to him, wouldn't you find it a bit suspicious that all of a sudden he has the money to buy a beauty like that?"

"He didn't pay for it himself. His girl loaned it to him."

"His girl? Which one?"

"Janet."

Killian laughed at the absurdity of that. "No way. Janet doesn't have that kind of money and even if she did, she wouldn't—"

"What do you know about her finances?" Gus asked, pacing in front of her. "About as much as I do, I'd wager, which is nothing."

"Did Cody or Janet tell you about this loan?"

"Cody."

"He didn't tell me that," Killian said, trying her best to keep her voice level. "He didn't say a thing about Janet loaning him the money."

"Maybe he didn't like the way you were asking."

She shook her head, refusing to be found at fault when she knew Cody was the one doing the double-talking. "He acted as if he'd paid for it himself. He said he got a good deal on it. In fact, he implied it was a steal."

"It *was* a good deal," Gus insisted. "He got an interest-free loan, didn't he?"

"I just don't know why he didn't tell me about this loan when he had the chance."

"Why should he? You've already decided he's guilty."

"Oh, Gus, that's not true and you know it. Look, we're both distraught and—"

"I'm not distraught," he said, hitching up his nose in an imitation of a blue blood, then he lowered his eyebrows to menace her. "I'm plain, old pissed off, lady."

"Well, join the club." She stepped right up to him, hands on her hips, anger seething beneath her skin. "I don't *want* the guilty party to be anyone in particular. I just want the truth. And where do you get off stomping into my place and yelling at me as if I'm one of your wranglers? You're not my boss, Breedlove," she said, punctuating the last few words with jabs of her finger to the center of his chest. He actually began backing away from her. "And you have no right to make demands on me or order me around. You got that, pal?"

"I came here to get some things straight. I'm not here to pick a fight, but you—"

"Get out!"

"Or what?" he asked, and although he wasn't smiling she sensed he was on the verge of it.

"I hope you'll leave without my having to make a scene."

"I'd like to see you throw me out. That would be mighty entertaining. Speaking of which . . ." He crossed his arms and rocked back on the heels of his boots. "Did you happen to catch *Entertainment World* this afternoon?"

"No, I wasn't near a television."

"They had a report on animal cruelty and guess whose name they dropped?"

"Oh, no." Killian realized she was shaking her head. "Not . . . they didn't say anything about—"

"August Breedlove," he interrupted. "Under current investigation for injuring a horse during a stunt for a Western being filmed in Oklahoma." He leaned closer to her. "So you're not the only one having a bad day, sweetheart. Couldn't you have at least gagged the press until you'd filed a report?"

"Gagged the press?" she repeated, incredulous. "You think I could do that, do you?" She laughed at the notion. "Even the President can't keep things out of the news. I'm sorry it leaked, but I had nothing to do with it."

"I might as well hang it up after this film. I'm ruined."

"Gus, you aren't." She placed a hand to her forehead and thought longingly of the aspirin scattered in the bathroom.

"Since my name has been dragged through the dirt, go ahead and trample the rest of me. I'll take the blame for it all. File your damned report and let's all put this behind us."

She didn't take him seriously at first, figuring he was only letting off steam. Then she met his unwavering gaze and the determination in his eyes made her gasp. "Gus, you're serious!"

"Dead serious," he assured her. "It won't be the first time I've had to start all over again." He dipped his head and his breath warmed her face. "Just lay off the kid, all right?"

"Gus, I don't take this lightly."

"You think I do?" He moved toward the door and swung it open. "I'm the one who has lost a good stunt horse. Gold Dollar will never work again because he's too spooked. I want to find out who hurt Gold Dollar, but not if it's going to destroy one career after another. Cody's just starting out. I don't want him ruined, you understand?"

"Even if he's the one who put Gold Dollar out of business?"

He ran a hand down his face and laughed, but she knew he wasn't amused. "What are you doing here? Playing with my head? You think Cody could actually do that—knowing how I would feel about it? You think he'd stab me in the back like that?"

"I think Cody doesn't think much, unfortunately. He's spontaneous. Impulsive. He goes off half-cocked."

"What about Bishop? He's clean as a hound's tooth?"

"No, I believe he ordered the trip-wire because he didn't want to wait for you to bring in another horse. But I can't prove any of this yet." She held up a hand before he could interrupt. "But I will, given enough time."

"I've run out of that. After that report on TV, my future looks pretty bleak."

"No, it isn't. I can't believe you'd throw yourself to the wolves and let the culprits get off scot-free?"

"Look, animal rights is a hot topic right now in California and nobody wants to hire someone who may get them into trouble or encourage people like you to come breathing down their necks."

She started to rail at him, but she spun away and put her hands over her face for a few moments while she reminded herself that she was a grown woman and not the type to scream like a banshee. "I'm not going to be put on the defensive and I'm not going to let you feed me a line of bull about the ruination of your career. This is not my first investigation, Gus. Other boss wranglers have discovered rotten apples on their payroll, but their reputations weren't destroyed over it. They're all still working—thriving."

"You don't understand . . ."

"Yes, I do. I understand that you're afraid Cody might be involved and that breaks your heart." She faced him again. He'd moved to stand just outside her motel room where shadow hid his features from her. "I won't let you take the rap for someone else."

"You really think it was him, don't you?"

"Cody's alibi has holes in it," she hedged. "Jerry Bishop is the type of man who looks for weaknesses in others just in case he can exploit them. It's beginning to add up."

Gus looked at her from beneath his eyebrows. "What did Bishop have to say?"

"Nothing much, but I don't like his attitude. He's too cocky for his own good. He acts like a man who's gotten away with manslaughter, so now he thinks he can get away with murder."

"He could have hired someone other than a wrangler or stuntman to do his dirty work."

"I know. I'm exploring all possibilities. I'm sorry Cody feels that I'm picking on him, but I'm not here to make friends, Gus. I'm here to right a wrong. Why is it so hard for you to even entertain the notion that Cody might have exercised poor judgment and—"

"He didn't."

"Gus, let Cody defend himself. Please don't make this more difficult by fighting his battles or by protecting him."

"I'm not protecting him. He didn't—" He shook his head and stepped off the concrete walkway. "I can see I'm not getting anywhere with you."

"Gus," Killian called after him, "I'm sorry about that TV report. I had nothing to do with it."

He stared at her for a long moment during which she couldn't tell if he believed her or not. Finally he strode to his truck and made tracks out of the parking lot. Killian closed the door and leaned back against it, her heart heavy.

What else could happen to her today? she wondered miserably. As if in answer, someone tapped at the door. She was loath to answer, but she forced herself to face the visitor. The wrangler standing outside was someone she had questioned briefly, but had eliminated from her list of suspects early on.

"Hello, Dan," she greeted him, noticing how nervous he was acting and how he couldn't even bring himself to look her in the eye. "Want to come in?"

"No." He cleared his throat and glanced from side to side and then behind him as if he thought he'd be attacked at any moment. "Did you see that TV show today?"

"Dan, I had nothing to do with that," she said, wondering if he was the first in a long line of cowboy visitors. Would they all come to her door and tell her she was a double-crossing publicity seeker?

"Gus is a good man. He had nothing to do with that horse getting hurt."

"I'm sure you're right. Look, I've had a long day and if I don't get into the shower soon—"

"Cody's not cut from the same cloth."

"Hello?" Killian said, her attention suddenly riveted to the cowboy with the downcast eyes. "What are you saying, Dan? Do you know something about Cody that I should know?"

"I'm the one who found Gold Dollar with his legs cut up, remember?"

"Yes," she said, recalling the interview she'd conducted with Dan Smithee. He'd gone in to feed the stock and had been the one who had first noticed the blood on Gold Dollar's legs.

"It had rained earlier that afternoon. There was mud all in the stall. Muddy bootprints. I heard that Janet Brubaker threw a hissy fit when Cody tracked in mud later that afternoon. She made him get a bucket and mop and clean up after himself. The other makeup girls thought that was a hoot."

"What else?" she urged, sensing he wasn't quite finished.

"The stuff in Gold Dollar's stall was red mud like over by the creek bank. You been out that way?"

"Yes, yesterday." With the exasperating August Breedlove, she tacked on mentally. In fact, she'd had to clean red mud stains off her boots and the knees of her jeans. "The ground is like clay by the creek and the trees are quite thick. It would be easy to stage something there on the sly."

"That's right. Now you're thinking. Red," he repeated. "Cody tracked in red mud. Ask Janet about it. She'll tell you. She's told everybody else."

"Thanks, Dan. I'll do that."

He touched the brim of his hat and began backing away. "I don't like singing canaries," he said. "But I don't like seeing good men ruined, either."

"Neither do I," Killian assured him, knowing they were both talking about the same man—Gus Breedlove.

5

BEING INSIDE Texas Pete's honky-tonk was like being inside a pinball machine: lights, whirring motion, and wall-to-wall earsplitting noise. Killian stood just inside the entrance and blinked owlishly, trying to adjust her eyes and ears. The place reeked of sweaty leather and foamy beer. A country-western band whipped the crowd into a two-step frenzy. Boot heels tapped the wooden dance floor and "Yeehaas" rose up as the song ended on a long, drawn-out chord.

She'd lived in the country most of her life and had spooned with her share of cowboys, but she'd never acquired a taste for country-western music or for tobacco-chewing good old boys. Easing around a hulking man with one cheek ballooned out and front teeth the color of coffee stains, she ignored his murmured, "Hey, sweet thing, let me buy you a beer."

She moved slowly through the crowd and found an empty space at the bar. Motioning for the bartender, she shook her head when the man next to her offered to pay for her drink.

"Yes'm? Light, dark, regular, low cal, wet or dry?" the barkeep asked, ready to pull her a brew.

"I'm looking for Cody Turnage. You know him?"

"Yep." He surveyed the crowd. "I believe he's over yonder. See that group of gals gathered up? He's most likely smack-dab in the middle of them."

Killian laughed knowingly. "I'm sure he is. Thanks." She wound her way around the tables toward the knot of rapt females. Sure enough, Cody sat at the table ringed by the laughing, flirting women. He held a knife in one hand and thrust it into his own chest. Gasps rose up, then Cody laughed and extracted the knife.

"Great, huh? The blade is rubber and it has a spring on it. When you shove it against something the blade goes into the handle." He demonstrated by shoving the blade against his palm. When he released it, the rubbery steel sprang back out. "So the next time you see somebody get knifed in the movies, y'all remember me." His laugh was a boyish hiccuping sound. When his gaze collided with Killian's, all the fun went out of him. He presented her with a disgusted expression and heaved a sigh that dripped with exasperation.

"Oh, hell. The chief inspector has tracked me down again."

"Good to see you, too," Killian said. "I need to talk to you, Cody."

"I'm socializing. See me tomorrow."

"No. Right now." She glanced around, looking for a better place for a serious chat. "Just you and me. It's important."

"Didn't my uncle talk to you?"

"Yes, and I told him to let you fight your own battles." She bent to whisper in his ear, "Act like a man, Cody, and quit hiding behind your Uncle Gus."

Her scolding did the trick. The color drained from Cody's face, making his freckles stand out even more. He sat back, tense as a bowstring, and then flicked a careless hand.

"This little lady wants my undivided attention and I won't have any peace until she gets it."

The others fell away, gliding off into the shadows, but glancing back curiously. Cody stared at the trick knife, rubbing his thumb along the dull blade.

"I know you've been asking questions about me all day," he said after a minute. "You talked to Janet and some of the other girls in the makeup trailer."

She could hardly hear him over the music, so she sat in the chair next to him, although he hadn't invited her. "You told Gus that Janet gave you the money to buy that saddle, but that's not true," Killian said, watching the pad of his thumb move up and down the knife blade. "Where did you get the money, Cody?"

"Maybe I saved it."

"And maybe you don't know truth from fiction, but I doubt it. Janet told me today about you tracking in mud—red mud like that near the creek."

"So what?" he said, sneering.

"She also said you weren't in the trailer the whole afternoon, but she can't say for sure how long you were gone. Might have been a few minutes, might have been a few hours." Killian shrugged. "How long was it, Cody? You tell me."

"Why should I? You're the college graduate. You figure it out. Besides, Janet is sore at me or she wouldn't be popping off. When she gets over her mad, she'll change her story again."

Killian took a tape recorder from her purse and placed it in the center of the table. Cody stared at it as if it were a rattlesnake. Killian switched on the machine. "Tell me, Cody. Somebody had to light the scene and somebody operated the camera. Who?"

"Not here." He pushed back his chair and stood up, then jerked his head to the right. "Back there in the poolroom. It's more private."

Grabbing the tape recorder and her purse, Killian followed him. Was he actually going to tell the truth? she wondered, anxious to see the end of this painful investigation. It would be lovely to have this thing over and done with, even if it meant leaving August Breedlove behind. She'd mark it off as one of those vicious jokes life played on the unsuspecting. First you're given someone like Gus, then fate rips him from your life before you can know the thrill of being with the right man at the right time and for the right reason.

She shoved such thoughts aside, afraid she might start crying in front of Cody. Half a dozen men stood around the two pool tables, but they paid Killian and Cody little attention. A row of chairs stood against one wall and Cody sat in the nearest one. Killian skipped a chair and put the tape recorder on the one between them. She punched one of the buttons on the side of the machine. Shifting her weight onto one hip, she twisted sideways to face Cody. He glared at the recorder, his eyes narrowed, his mouth thin beneath his sparse mustache.

"You think film was shot?" he asked. "Show it to me."

Killian frowned. So he wasn't going to make it easy, she thought with dread. Well, she was in the back room with the boys, so she'd have to play by their hardball rules. Putting an edge to her voice, she almost hissed at Cody. "Listen, kid, you know as well as I do that whatever film was shot was destroyed. Of course, if you'd gotten away with it, that scene would have been used—showcased even. Must have looked spectacular with that horse suddenly pitching forward, screaming and rolling and fighting against the pain while the rider was thrown clear. Must have been one great stunt on film." She stared at him, but he refused to meet her gaze. "I'd congratulate you, but the words stick in my throat."

"It's only a movie," he mumbled.

"What did you say?" Killian asked, wanting him to repeat that unfeeling remark.

"It's only a movie," he repeated. "It's not like this is grand jury stuff, you know. Stunts are stunts. They're not international intrigue, for Pete's sake. Hell, you act as if somebody got murdered or something."

"No one was murdered, but a living creature was maimed," she pointed out. "You're right about movies not being that important. Certainly not important enough to justify torturing animals."

"Torturing?" he asked, his eyes blazing with sudden anger. "Gold Dollar's going to be fine. He's not maimed and nobody tortured him."

"He's nearly lame," she corrected, then decided to throw him a curve. "Bishop says you're the most likely wrangler to have rigged the wire." It was a lie, but she was desperate.

Cody stared at her for a few seconds and then he looked at the trick knife he held. He rammed the blade back into the handle and let it spring out three times. When his eyes met hers again, she knew he hadn't bitten. He's a pretty good liar himself, she thought, and it takes one to know one.

"I don't believe you. Bishop didn't say anything like that. You're trying to pen me in and make me say something stupid."

"Are you going to take responsibility for this all by yourself?" Killian asked, refusing to back off. "Bishop says you're eager to please. He told me that you might have heard him complaining about not being able to get the effect he wanted and you rigged the wire to impress him." Part of that was true, but most of it was fabricated.

Cody shook his head, smiling. "He didn't say that."

Damn, Killian thought. Was he bluffing or was she that rotten a liar? "Maybe he didn't say it to you, but he said it to me."

"You're making all this up."

She shrugged, but was ashamed of herself. She forced herself to remember how deep the cuts were on Gold Dollar's front legs and her resolve returned. "I'm only repeating what I was told."

"So I had mud on my boots. Big deal."

"You have a fancy new saddle, too," Killian reminded him.

"I got a good deal on it. I told you that."

"I spoke to the cowboy you bought the saddle from, Cody. You paid top dollar."

"That guy doesn't work with the company anymore," he said, the information bursting from him. "Now I *know* you're lying."

Killian smiled briefly, glad she'd done her research on this point. "He's working in Dallas and I phoned him." She angled closer to study Cody's wavering certainty. "Did you think he'd lie for you, Cody? Do you think everyone is as loyal as your uncle? Bishop isn't. Bishop is out for himself, and if he can escape by sacrificing you, he'll do it." She sat away from him, but made sure he heard her next words. "He's already done it." Earlier, she'd pressed the hold button on the recorder, hoping to make Cody believe she'd turned it on so that now, when she pressed the button again to let the tape run, he would think she'd switched it off. Glancing at him, she saw him relax. She'd fooled him. "Bishop said he had no idea you'd rigged a wire until it was too late."

"Bull!" Cody faced the front and stared moodily at the men playing pool. "He knew. It was his idea. He said he used a trip-wire in another film years ago and that the horse wasn't hurt. Just a little shook up, you know, but not hurt."

"You knew better than that, Cody," Killian chided. "You knew that a trip-wire would hurt a horse."

"I didn't study it all that much. Bishop offered me the money and I figured if I turned him down, he'd find somebody else to take it. Hell, the wranglers and stunt-men aren't a chorus of angels."

"Who shot the film?"

"Bishop. It was just him and me. That scene was a simple setup. The good guy was supposed to ride right at the camera and his horse would be shot out from under him. Bishop couldn't get the effect he wanted and that's why Uncle Gus went to get Apache. Apache is better at falling and rolling than Gold Dollar."

"But Bishop couldn't wait."

"Time is money," Cody said, repeating an oft-used excuse on movie sets. "That's what Bishop said. Time is money. I figured I could do the stunt and Gold Dollar wouldn't get too roughed up."

"Oh, please," Killian said, moaning and not bothering to hide her disgust.

"I swear," Cody insisted. "I didn't expect the wire to cut so deep. It scared me, I tell you. I couldn't stop the bleeding and Bishop didn't give a damn."

"So you just put Gold Dollar in his stall and left him there to bleed," Killian said, bringing her gaze around to meet Cody's. He grimaced and his eyes pleaded for mercy, but Killian refused to show him any. "Have you no conscience?"

"There was nothing I could do and I couldn't hang around the stables. I knew Dan Smithee would be along to feed the stock and he'd know what to do for Gold Dollar."

"And you had your money, so what if a horse bled a little, right?" Killian picked up the recorder and switched it off.

"Hey, was that thing on?"

She nodded and tucked it inside her purse. "That's right, bucko. You're on tape."

He bounded to his feet, assuming a threatening stance, the prop knife clutched in one fist. "None of it was my fault. Bishop told me to do it."

"What did he do, put a knife to your throat?" she asked, glancing at the fake one. "You're a big boy, Cody. Don't you think it's time you started acting like one?"

"I just did what my boss told me to do."

"And you took bonus money for it."

"I was paid for my work, so what?" His voice cracked like a young boy's. "Bishop's the one you should write up. I just did what I was told."

"So you keep saying," Killian noted, growing cold inside the more Cody tried to wriggle out of admitting poor judgment and an appalling lack of integrity. "You have no will of your own, is that what you're telling me? No spine? No guts? Somebody tells you to do something, waves greenbacks in your face and you have to obey orders."

"No, but—"

"Cody," she said, twisting around so that she was face-to-face with him, "when are you going to start accepting responsibility for your own actions?"

"You talk as if I murdered someone."

"You broke the rules. You hurt an innocent animal."

He shoved the movie knife into his back pocket. "You're making a federal case out of this. Hell, Uncle Gus is the one who showed me how to rig a wire. Why don't you try this sermon on him?"

"He *taught* you?" Killian asked, rising from the chair to face Gus's accuser. "You expect me to believe that Gus—"

"You're going to tell him about me, aren't you?"

She puffed out a sigh, staggered by Cody's total lack of remorse. "Yes, unless you'd rather—"

"No, you go ahead." He grinned and ducked his head like the proverbial bad boy. "He'll take it better from you. He's going to bust a gut when he finds out it was me, but he'll get over it. He knows this business and what you have to do to get ahead in it." A spate of laughter floated into the room and Cody looked longingly toward the crowded bar. "It feels good to get it off my chest. I think I'll go kick up my heels now that I've confessed." He closed one eye in a jaunty wink. "Thanks for pleading my case to Uncle Gus. I owe you."

"Cody, I think you should tell him yourself. This is serious and it should come from you."

"Yeah, I'll think about it. Maybe if I get drunk enough tonight . . . naw, you tell him for me." Cody sauntered away from her and melted into the pool of bodies in the other room.

Leaving by the back way, Killian went to her car and drove it straight to Gus's trailer. She dreaded telling him about Cody, but knew it had to be done. She owed that to him. After another few moments of mentally rehearsing how she'd deliver the bad news, she knocked on the storm door.

"Yeah, who's there?" Gus called out.

"Killian. I have to speak to you," she added, thinking that he might try to evade her. After all, their last meeting hadn't ended sweetly or even cordially.

Gus propped open the storm door. "What's up?" he asked, none too politely.

"May I come in?"

"Well, I . . ." He glanced over his shoulder. Past him, Killian saw Janet Brubaker. For a blazing, irrational moment, Killian felt the heat of jealousy flare within her. "I have company."

"That's okay," Janet said grabbing up her purse and jacket. "Thanks for listening, Gus. I'll be going now."

"I could come back later," Killian offered half-heartedly.

"No, that's okay. I've got to find Cody anyway. He's probably chomping at the bit, wondering where I am."

"He's at Texas Pete's."

"He is? He's supposed to be in his trailer waiting for me."

"I just saw him at Texas Pete's," Killian said, shrugging helplessly.

"What have you been doing, following him?" Gus asked.

Facing him, Killian warned herself not to be drawn into an argument, but she was finding it hard to control herself. "Let's talk inside. Please?"

He motioned her inside, then he waved to Janet. "See you later. Glad you stopped by, Janet. If you see Cody, remind him that we have a seven o'clock call in the morning."

Killian sat on the edge of the couch and wished Gus would sit next to her. He seemed rooted to his position in front of the door.

"You have been following Cody, haven't you?" He closed the wood door and turned slowly until his hooded gaze met hers. "You're damned determined to nail him, aren't you?"

"What was Janet doing here?" Why did she ask that? she wondered, then called herself a few choice names. She knew why. She was fighting off jealousy.

He sent her a baffled glance. "Where do you come off questioning me about my guests?"

"Did she come here to talk about Cody?"

"You want a drink?" he asked, padding barefoot to the kitchen. "I've got beer, whiskey, cola, tomato juice—"

"Tomato juice." She hurried after him. "Did she tell you something about Cody that I should know?"

He handed her a small can of juice. "Want a glass?"

"No."

"She told me that she admitted to you that Cody wasn't in the makeup trailer the entire afternoon. She feels bad about having lied to you, but she's crazy about Cody and she wanted to protect him."

"She's not the only one who wants to protect him."

"Meaning me?" he asked, pouring himself a glass of milk. "Family sticks together."

"Even through lying and breaking the rules?"

His gaze slipped to hers with the keenness of a knife blade. "If you have something to tell me, then tell me."

"I think you're way ahead of me," she noted, sensing his rigid control. If ever there was a man prepared for a blow, it was him. "I'm sorry, Gus."

He drank some of the milk, then turned away from her to stare out the window above the kitchen sink. "The little runt did it, huh?"

"Yes. I have it on tape, if you'd like—"

"Did he say why?"

"Bishop paid him a bonus."

"That's how he bought the saddle."

"Did Janet tell you that she didn't loan him the money?"

"Yes." He looked at the half-filled glass and then poured the remaining milk into the sink. "Well, you got your man." His voice was tight, narrow, as if he was speaking through clenched teeth.

"I got my *men*. I'm going to write up Bishop, too."

"And me?"

"You?" She touched his shoulder. He stiffened. "Why would I write you up? You haven't done anything . . . have you?" She waited, wanting him to confirm his innocence. When he edged away from her to go back into the living room, Killian beat down an absurd urge to cry. Why was she so emotional lately? For days she'd been on the verge of tears countless times. It was as if she was battling an overwhelming sadness, barely keeping it at bay. She suspected her odd mood had a lot to do with her disappointment that she and Gus hadn't been able to stay on friendly terms. But it was more than that. She was frustrated. God help her, she was sexually frustrated. She'd always prided herself on being interested in, but not obsessed with, the opposite sex. Breedlove had changed that.

She set the can of juice on the counter and went to find Gus. Sitting in a leather recliner, he had covered the lower part of his face with one hand. His eyes said it all—he was shattered by her news.

"Are you going to be okay?" Killian asked, taking hesitant steps toward him.

"I wouldn't blame you for thinking that I knew Cody tripped that horse and I kept my mouth shut about it."

"Gus, I don't—"

"Where did you say Cody was?" He rose from the chair and reached for a jean jacket draped over the back of the couch. "Texas Pete's?"

"Yes. He was—"

"I've got to talk to him." He pulled keys from his pocket. "So, if you don't mind . . ."

"Here's your hat, what's your hurry," Killian sassed, aggravated by his refusal to let her console him. "Gus, I wish Cody hadn't been involved. I know how much you love him and want the best—"

"Can you save this until later? I really want to catch up with Cody tonight."

"Fine." She retrieved her purse and marched outside ahead of him. "If you want to treat me as if I'm your enemy, go right ahead. I had a job to do and I did it."

"This has nothing to do with you," he said in a condescending tone. "You've delivered your news. Thanks for giving it to me straight."

She stood before him, wanting to bury herself in his arms and take away some of the grief she knew was consuming him. But he was as inviting as a marble statue.

"Gus, he'll have to be suspended immediately. If you don't, then I—"

"You think I'd let him near my livestock again after he's confessed to hurting one of my horses?" he asked, anger shaking his voice. He moved quickly to his pickup, almost bowling over her. "I'm not going looking for him in order to console him. I'm going to find him and tell him to pack up his gear and clear out." He climbed into the truck and started the engine. "Then I'm going to try to get out of my contract."

"Gus, no!" She reached inside the truck window and grabbed a handful of his jacket sleeve. "You can't—"

"I don't want to work for Bishop another day if I can help it." He eased his sleeve from her fingers. "I wouldn't be surprised if Bishop rigged the wire."

"Cody has already confessed that he did that. He said you showed him how."

Gus's gaze swung around to her in a test of wills.

"That's what he said, Gus. I'm only repeating—"

"I'll thank you not to repeat it again—to anyone." His lips were white with rage, his words clipped. "Watch out." Then he gunned the motor and left her standing in a cloud of dust.

KILLIAN WENT BACK to Gus's trailer the next morning, feeling like a criminal returning to the scene of the crime. As she approached she heard Cody's voice through the open window. She stopped, wondering if she should come back when Gus was alone, but the next voice was Gus's and what he said rooted her to the spot.

"You think I'll sweet-talk Killian into going easy on you? Think again, Cody. She doesn't trust me anyway. Thanks to you, she probably has serious doubts about my judgment."

"She likes you. I can tell," Cody insisted, his tone bordering on a whine. "Just tell her this is my first offense and that I'm real sorry—"

"You tell her."

"It'll sound better coming from you."

"Uh-uh. If you want to talk to her, you'd better shake a leg. Now that she knows what went down, she'll leave for Oklahoma City to file her report. She might have left already."

"Uncle Gus, come on. All you have to do is just tell her I'm not a bad guy. I listened to the wrong boss. She'll understand if you explain it to her. After all, she doesn't want to sleep with *me*."

Killian gasped, wanting to slap Cody, but then she heard a grunt and realized Gus had beat her to it.

"Oww! What the hell did you hit me for?" Cody asked, whining for real now.

"Because you're a jackass, that's why. I'm through defending your tarnished honor, kid. For once in your life, stand up on your hind legs and act like a man. Take your punishment and then straighten out your life. I've got problems of my own. We all have problems."

"Everybody knows you're clean as the driven snow."

"Not everyone. Some people haven't forgotten that other trouble I had and this has only stirred up the rumors again."

"Uncle Gus, I'm sorry—"

"Save it. You can't con me anymore, Cody. I trusted you. I believed in you, but no more. Until you prove to me you've changed for the better, I don't want to hear your excuses and I'm sure as hell not going to plead for your mercy. And for your information, you've got it backward. She doesn't want to sleep with me, *I* want to sleep with *her*. I don't expect you to understand, but there's a big difference."

Amazed, Killian turned and went toward her car. Her eavesdropping had left her uncomfortably warm and unquestionably titillated. She decided to sneak off and come back a little while later when the scene was less explosive, but most of her awareness was taken up with the implications of the confession she'd just heard. Gus wanted to sleep with her, but he wasn't sure the feeling was mutual.

And he was right. She *would* be leaving soon—today, tomorrow at the latest. But she didn't want to leave without hope. She didn't want him to think she wasn't deeply attracted to him, agonizingly aware of him.

Killian opened the car door and was about to settle into the front seat when Gus and Cody stepped outside. She stood, caught in the act, and could think of nothing else to do but close the car door and offer a weak smile.

Cody was still wearing what he'd had on last night at Texas Pete's, but Gus had stripped down to unbuttoned jeans and a white undershirt. He buttoned his jeans quickly, modestly. Killian found herself hoping he wouldn't go back inside and put on a shirt. She liked the way the sleeveless, ribbed undershirt clung to him and left naked his muscled arms and wide neck.

"Good morning," she said, still standing beside her car, unsure of her timing.

"Good morning. We were just talking about you," Gus said, then glared at his nephew. "Cody wanted to tell you something."

"Oh, what's that?"

At first Cody scowled, but turned on the charm when he faced Killian. "I just wanted you to know there's no hard feelings. I know I did wrong. I shouldn't have listened to Bishop, but he acted like I'd be doing him this big favor and—"

"Pardon me," Gus said, a slur in his voice. "But I've already heard these mealymouthed excuses and I'm sick to death of them." He went back inside and slammed the front door.

Cody had the decency to blush. His laugh was hollow, uneasy. "He's right. There isn't an excuse good enough for what I did. I knew better. I was wrong. I admit it. So, fry me."

"I'm not out to fry anyone," Killian said, feeling a twinge of pity for him. "I hope you've learned that it's best to be honest. If you'd only confessed up-front, you could have saved everyone a lot of pain and problems. I think your uncle is more upset by the fact you lied to him than that you showed poor judgment in taking bonus money to do something you knew was wrong."

"I didn't think Gold Dollar would get all banged up. Uncle Gus told me that trip-wires were used all the time in the old days."

"And their use was banned because horses were maimed by them. Many broke their legs on those wires. It's a wonder Gold Dollar didn't." Killian sighed, shaking her head at Cody's feeble evasions. "Do you understand how wrong you were?"

"Yeah, yeah. Uncle Gus has already read the riot act to me, so you can spare me." He shoved his cowboy hat onto his head and swaggered away from her. "I've got to pack. See you around, hon. Gold Dollar still likes me. Hope you do, too." Whistling a merry tune, he climbed into his dusty pickup and roared away.

"Killian?"

She spun around to find Gus standing in the doorway of his trailer. "Yes?"

"Would you come inside for a minute?"

"S-sure." Her voice broke on the word, a victim of a sudden bout of nerves. He looked so virile in that undershirt and those old, faded, threadbare jeans. So sexy. How could she leave without knowing what it would be like to let him make love to her? She went up the steps and he took one of her hands in his and pulled her inside. He closed the door and Killian found herself flattened against it as he moved up to her, so close his body seemed to melt into hers.

"Wh-what's this all about?" she asked, her voice cracking again as she stared directly at the desire flaring in his eyes. Her hands rested against his waist and she slipped her fingertips under the loose band of his jeans.

"I want to kiss you goodbye," he said, his eyes drifting down to her mouth. Tension radiated from him—sexual tension. It vibrated in the air around them; it charged the atmosphere.

"Gus, should we...why..." She shook her head, trying to sling her thoughts into order. If only things had been different for them, she thought. A beautiful sadness came over her and brought tears to her eyes. "I only wish we could have . . ."

"Me, too, but it's not too late. Let's grant that wish." His lips brushed hers and the spark became a flame. Suddenly she was in his arms, exchanging hot kisses, murmuring his name with an urgency she'd never known before.

She abandoned everything: her pride, her doubts, herself. All she had left was her passion and for now that was enough.

6

THE SHEER POWER OF HIS DESIRE shocked him. Swaying back, Gus stared into Killian's upturned face and his heart swelled with longing. Her shimmering, blond hair felt fine and soft against his fingers as he stroked the wisps from her forehead. He kissed her left temple and the scent of her perfume filled his head.

"You're having second thoughts," she whispered. "I understand."

"No, I'm not, and no, you don't." Framing her sweet face in his hands, he remembered the rainy night at the motel when he'd first met her—how his heart had stood still, how her smile had jump-started it. She'd looked like a landlocked mermaid, raindrops slipping down her cheeks to the corners of her alluring mouth. He'd wanted her then as he wanted her now. While circumstances had conspired to make her his enemy, they had never diminished his hunger for her company, his craving for her touch.

"I'm leaving this afternoon to file my report and—"

"I don't want to talk about reports or goodbyes or anything like that," he said, hearing the impatience in his voice, feeling it burn between his thighs. "Let's be selfish." He rubbed his mouth against hers, smearing her lipstick, licking it off her lips. Her arms slipped around his waist. Her gaze fastened on his mouth. "To hell with your job and mine. To hell with investigations and other people's problems and excuses." He kissed her, hard and quick. "I don't think I can let you leave without . . ." He rocked his hips forward and pressed himself against her. "I've just got to have you, Killian."

A moan escaped her a second before she surged up to meet his open mouth. Her tongue swept inside in a wild, anxious search. He tamed it with his own, thrusting deep, making her quiver and moan again. He bent his knees and wrapped his arms just below her shapely bottom, then he lifted her off the ground and carried her to the bedroom. Her mouth never left his and her tongue whipped him into a frenzy. He let go of her and she slipped down his body and lay back on the quilted bedspread, a sexy invitation.

Passion glazed his vision, softening corners, making everything vibrate as if waves of heat were rising off the bedding, off her. He stretched out on top of her, full of his own primal need to dominate and conquer. He sprinkled quick kisses over her face.

He sat up, straddling her. She smiled, eager and confident. She wasn't afraid or demure and this heightened his excitement. He ripped off his undershirt. Snaking her hands up over his chest, she delved through the hair there, and massaged his nipples.

Her eyes spoke volumes, telling him she wanted more—she wanted all he had to give. Then things soared out of control and he acted on pure instinct, giving himself over to his selfish core.

"Unbutton me," he said, his throat so thick he could hardly speak. He sounded like a greedy man, but he didn't care, especially when her trembling fingers bumped against the front of his jeans and freed the buttons one by one. He laid open her blouse. Her bra was flesh-colored, sheer, sexy.

Like a starving man, he fastened his mouth over one of her breasts and wet the shiny fabric thoroughly. Her nipple poked at his tongue and Killian arched up. Her hands grasped his head, holding fast, transmitting back to him the pleasure he'd given. Finding the front clasp he unfastened her bra, peeled it off, slung it across the room. Her breasts filled his eager hands. He flicked his thumbs over her puckered, pink areolas and blushing nipples, then took one in his mouth, drawing in as much as he could to suckle and kiss. She released her breath in a slow hiss. Her fingers massaged his scalp and mussed his hair.

"God, you're so beautiful."

"Oh, Gus," she whispered, smiling, her eyes tearing.

Tenderness for her swamped him. He nuzzled her soft-skinned breasts and traced the blue veins just beneath her skin with the tip of his tongue. She trembled and made a cradle for him, opening her legs, hooking her heels at the back of his thighs. She tugged at the waistband of his jeans and he helped her push them down over his hips.

"You're the beautiful one," she murmured, stroking him, admiring his erection. She ran her hands over his buttocks, up his spine, over his shoulders. He thought he would die.

"Let me...I've got a couple of..." He shook his head, having trouble making sense when her hands were on him. Leaning past her, he jerked open a drawer, felt around and finally found the little foil package. "Wait, honey. Let me get this . . . thing on."

"How sweet." She smiled and his heart melted. "Allow me," she said, taking the foil from him and tearing it open.

Her hands were cool on his hot flesh, but sure and steady. His need for her blasted through him. He inched her jeans and silky panties down over her hips and slim legs, then he moved on top of her again. This time it was far more pleasurable. Her skin slipped against his. Every part of him tingled in response to the delicate thrill of female flesh. His tongue mated with hers, imitating what another part of him strained to do. She moaned and the sound filled his head, when he realized he was moaning, too. She shifted as if searching for a way to connect. He obliged and guided himself into her. She was warm and wet. He closed his eyes, overcome with the divine pleasure of being one with her. After nights of dreaming, after days of fantasizing, he and Killian were a reality.

He was glad he'd abandoned his notions of what was right, wrong, honorable, dishonorable, prudent, imprudent. All that mattered to him was to get all the way inside her and stay there, to feel her clutch him, to know that she shared his glory, his climax.

Her mouth was so sweet under his, so tender and giving. She whispered his name and her breath soughed across his hot face. The driving force inside him crested, taking him by surprise, obliterating all thought of her for a few shattering, heart-exploding moments. He was a taut bowstring suddenly plucked and left to quiver, playing a one-note song all his own. Then he felt his own release and heard Killian's answering cries, but most of his awareness was taken up with the brisk evaporation of his pent-up longing. It seemed to escape through every pore of his body and leave him light-headed, free-hearted, reborn.

"Don't go," she said, gripping his hips and holding fast. "I don't want us to end yet."

The profound poignancy of that reality sent a spear of comprehension through him. He'd hoped this might be a beginning for them, but she'd just told him it was not to be. This was goodbye, after all.

GUS TIPTOED OUT of the bathroom, but then he saw that Killian was awake.

"I must have dozed off," she said, propping herself up on her elbows and blinking her eyes rapidly. "Why are you dressed?"

"I'm only half-dressed," he pointed out, motioning to his jeans, then bare feet and chest. "You were asleep, so . . ." Damn her, why was she looking at him as if he'd left a fifty on the pillow? "You said earlier that you had to go."

"Well, yes, but not this minute." She tugged the sheet up under her arms. "But if I'm in the way . . ."

"You're not." He sighed. This wasn't going well. How could two people be so graceful in bed and so awkward out of it?

"I thought we could snuggle awhile," she said, sounding hurt. "I do have to leave, but I was looking forward to a few goodbye kisses." She smiled sexily. "And not just on my lips."

Sealed with a kiss... parting is such sweet sorrow...absence makes the heart grow fonder. What crap! He couldn't help feeling sorry for himself for losing her so soon after he'd finally found her—the real her. The one who could not only drive him wild with desire but satisfy him as no other woman ever had.

Suddenly, she jerked the sheet off the bed with her and stomped toward him. "I'm taking a shower. Do you mind?"

"No, go right ahead." He moved aside before she could bulldoze him down like so much rubble. She slammed the bathroom door just in case he had any stupid ideas of joining her.

Sitting on the edge of the bed, Gus pulled on his T-shirt and listened to the sting of water on the shower tiles. He knew it was up to him to smooth this over and make the parting as painless as possible, but knowing wasn't enough. His gut burned with unjustified anger. Damn her, why did she have to leave just when things were so great between them? He wasn't any good at long goodbyes.

Plowing his hands through his hair, he grimaced when he heard her turn off the water. Maybe he should play it cool, he thought. Tell her it was great and see her to the door. That wasn't his style, either, but he couldn't think straight. If it had been any other woman, he wouldn't be agonizing over his attitude and hers. But she wasn't any other woman. She was Killian. And the moment he'd plunged himself into her, he'd known that he was lost inside her, and lost to any other woman for a long, long time.

Killian emerged from the bathroom like a woman possessed. Grabbing her clothes off the floor and furniture, she moved with a checked fury Gus couldn't help but admire.

"You're angry, right?" he asked as she tugged on her jeans.

"How observant."

"Look, I didn't mean to hurt your feelings. I just thought that you'd sleep and then be in a big hurry to get going."

"Oh, is that what you thought?" She buttoned her blouse. "*I'd* be in a big hurry."

"Yes." He stood up and closed his hands over her shoulders. The curve of her neck tempted him and he bent his head to press his lips to the softness of her skin. She smelled of Irish Spring. "It's nothing to do with you or what we did. I'm just no good at saying goodbye."

"Nothing personal, huh?" she asked, spinning around to glare at him with teary eyes.

"Hey, what's this? You're crying." He felt emotion lodge in his throat. God, he'd never meant to make her cry! He raked a hand through his hair, feeling totally out of control.

"You're damned right, I'm crying." She stepped into her loafers and pushed her hair back from her face. "And you're to blame for that."

"Why? What did I do? Just because I put on my jeans while you were asleep?"

"*Please*," she said dryly.

"What then?"

"Your attitude." She spun around and marched toward the front door, grabbing her purse on the way.

"What about it?" Gus asked, following behind her like a lost lamb.

"It stinks!" She wrenched the door open and then turned sideways to burn him to a crisp with the heat of her glittering eyes. "You act as if we just shook hands. *We made love.* Or, at least, I did. I guess what you were doing was getting your jollies."

Her anger sparked his. "Hold on just a damned minute." He grabbed the side of the door to keep her from opening it any farther. "You're the one who was so all-fired anxious to say goodbye. I thought that's what you were doing in bed with me. Kissing me off!"

"Wh-what?" She looked stunned for a moment, then her eyes hardened and the tears dried up. "Oh, no, you don't. You're not going to make me feel lousy. My motives were pure. I made love to you because you wanted me and I wanted you. I couldn't leave without loving you, and you told me the same thing, so don't stand there and pretend you were in the dark about what we were doing in your bed!" She surprised him with her strength by pushing the door and him back far enough to allow her to step outside. "But if you want me to kiss you off, you've got it, pal. Goodbye!" She flung the word in his face. "And good riddance," she tacked on.

"Killian, don't go like this..." He didn't think she heard him, she was so filled with her own fury, her own pain. But she glanced back at him, eyes so full of accusations they stung him like darts.

"I should have left right after you'd finished with me, I suppose," she said bitterly. "I've never been a cheap lay before."

"Killian!" He started after her, but she was as quick as a rabbit and was in her car and peeling rubber before he could hobble barefoot down the steps and into the yard. "I never wanted to say goodbye," he said lamely. Then he limped toward the trailer, feeling like a damned fool. A fool for love.

SUMMER WAS IN FULL BLAZE across Oklahoma. Spring's gentle rain and cool breezes had given way to days of humid heat.

Gus sat on the top rail of the wood fence and watched a seasoned mare tease an untried stallion. He chuckled, amused at the stallion's ineptness and the mare's obvious impatience. His attention switched from the mismatched couple to the silver pickup stirring dust as it bumped along the road toward him. It was his sister May, he thought, lifting an arm over his head to wave grandly at her. She was his closest neighbor, leasing a spread a couple of miles away.

May Turnage bounded out of the pickup. She was a small woman, and most of her black hair had turned silver. She was ten years older than Gus, but treated him like a big brother, coming to him often for advice and guidance. Life had etched deep lines around her eyes and she'd lost most of her youthful vibrancy—a victim of widowhood and a son who was often more trouble than he was worth.

"What's going on here?" she asked, eyeing the two horses in the corral. "You trying Rebel Rouser out on Julia's Pride?"

"I thought Julia's Pride might be good for him. She's never played hard to get and he needs encouragement the first time around. Look at him. Still as awkward as a colt. I don't think he'll ever be grace in motion."

"No, but I bet he'll throw off some fine-looking colts." May took Gus's hand and he pulled her up to sit next to him on the rail. "How old is Julia's Pride?"

"Twelve. She's getting up there."

"She's got a few years of colt-bearing left. She's healthy."

"So, what brings you out here in the middle of the day?" Gus asked, knowing this was usually a busy time for May. She also raised horses, but spent most of her time boarding and training other people's. City people, mostly, who didn't mind paying big money to keep their horses at the ready for their occasional riding whims.

"Have you seen Cody?" she asked. "I was hoping he'd be here," she added when Gus shook his head.

"He's missing?"

"He didn't come home last night."

"May, when are you going to give up trying to make that son of yours a Boy Scout? If you don't want to worry about him night after night, tell him to move out."

"I'm always afraid he's in a hospital or—"

"If he's laid up, he's most likely laid up with some blonde in town or in Tulsa . . . or Broken Arrow." An image of himself sprawled out in bed with Killian tore a chunk from his heart. He sucked in his breath sharply and averted his face from May, not willing to share his private misery.

"Gus?" May placed a hand on his forearm. "Did something happen at that last job?"

"Besides Cody screwing up royally, you mean?"

"Yes, besides that."

"No," he said, shaking off the melancholy and the memory of how badly he'd behaved toward Killian. She'd wanted a long, mushy goodbye, but he couldn't stomach it. He'd been too brusque, too aloof. He'd gotten exactly what he'd deserved—a broken heart.

"Gus?" May jiggled his arm. "What's wrong, hon? You've been so moody since you got back."

He heaved a restless sigh. "Nothing. I just hope that investigation won't stir up more trouble for me. I've cleaned up my reputation over the past few years, but this will jar memories and hand my enemies new ammunition."

"What enemies?" May asked, shaking her head. "I never heard anything but good about you. You blew that whole situation out of proportion. If you'd only have stuck to your guns and not run off like some—"

"I know, I know," he said, cutting her off because he'd heard this lecture so many times before. "But I did what I did. It's over—or so I thought."

"Has someone brought up your past?"

"No." He frowned, wondering if he was worrying over nothing. "But I'm expecting it. I think I'll get out of the film business altogether."

"Oh, Gus." She wrapped her hands around his upper arm and leaned her head against his shoulder. Her sadness for him brought a wedge of emotion to his throat. "I'm sorry Cody has caused you so much grief."

"It's not your fault."

"There's something else . . ."

"What?" he asked, looking down into her hazel eyes.

"You tell me," she said, smiling. "Cody told me that you and that lady investigator had a thing going. Have you seen her since the film wrapped?"

"No. That's history." He shrugged, trying for nonchalance. "It's the nature of the business. You get all close and palsy-walsy, then the work is over and everyone goes their separate ways."

She pulled away, trying to read the expression on his face. He tried not to show her anything, but she'd known him all his life and could usually see right through him.

"If you like her so much, why not go see her?"

"Who said I liked her?" He glanced at his sister. She was looking at him as if he'd just denied he was a man. He laughed at the futility of trying to lie to a woman who had him down cold. "The lady wants it this way."

"She said she didn't want to see you again?"

"She said goodbye. Means the same thing."

"Not always. Where does she live?"

"Broken Arrow."

"Broken Arrow!" May popped his shoulder with her fist. "You stubborn cuss. The gal lives twenty minutes from here and you're so full of pride you can't drag yourself that short distance? You deserve to be alone, August Brian Breedlove."

"Thanks, sis. Your pep talk has made me feel downright chipper," he drawled with pointed sarcasm.

"Gus, you know I'm telling you this for your own good."

His glance questioned her goodwill and she cuffed him again, this time grazing his chin with her knuckles.

"If you're thinking about her after...how many weeks has it been since you've seen her?"

"Six," he said, realizing too late that his quick answer had given him away.

May laughed. "But who's counting, right?" She bumped shoulders with him, making him smile. "If you're still thinking about her after six weeks, for heaven's sake, go see her. Are you afraid she'll bounce you on your ear?"

"No. I just don't want to horn in on her life if she'd rather not see me again." He studied his hands for a moment, not really seeing them. "I don't think she trusts me."

"Why do you think that?"

He shrugged, trying to escape the weight of indecision. "Why should she? I was head wrangler and her investigation turned up some ugly goings-on."

"None of that was your fault."

"I showed Cody how to rig a trip-wire. He told her about it. She'd be a fool not to wonder if I was really so squeaky-clean." He looked at his sister when her silence extended past the moment. Her forehead was wrinkled with worry and she chewed on a fingernail. Ever since her teenage years, she'd manicured her nails that way when she was nervous, which was far too often. "Quit chewing your nails," he admonished in the same tone his mother had used countless times.

She sat on her hands. "Why did you show Cody how to rig a wire?"

"He asked about it and I demonstrated. At the time, I didn't think anything of it. I thought it was a good lesson, showing him how the wire could put down a horse. He asked me if many horses were hurt. I told him what I'd always heard, that some wranglers knew tricks to ensure that the horses weren't hurt, but it wasn't guaranteed. More often than not, the horses were bruised or cut. You know Cody. He hears what he wants to hear and conveniently forgets the rest."

"Yes, he's got a lot of bad habits and that's one of them," May agreed. "But about this woman . . . people learn to trust, Gus. She sure won't learn to trust you long-distance."

The stallion suddenly mounted the mare and May jabbed Gus in the ribs with her elbow. They watched in respectful silence as the two horses mated, executing a shuffling, almost savage dance. The mare laid back her lips, exposing her teeth. The stallion let out a cry of release, then fell away and staggered.

"Knocked him silly," May said, laughing. "I think he liked it."

Gus nodded, laughing too hard to answer. Rebel Rouser recovered and pranced around the corral, flinging his head and kicking up his heels. Julia's Pride watched him for a minute, then sauntered to the water trough for a drink.

"Wouldn't hurt to drop in and say howdy to that gal in Broken Arrow, would it?"

"I reckon not," Gus said, shifting on the fence rail, uncomfortable with the sudden tightness in the front of his jeans.

"What's her name?"

"Killian." Just saying her name made his passion rise. He slid off the fence. "Killian Whittier."

"Beautiful name. Does it fit her?"

He pulled rawhide over his hands and smiled. "Like a glove."

"I'M BACK," Killian called as she entered through the back door of the veterinary clinic. Her father stepped out from one of the examination rooms, looking decidedly miffed.

"I thought you were going to lunch," Sam Whittier said, hands akimbo, thick white eyebrows knitted in a frown.

"That's right."

"That was three hours ago."

"I stopped by the library," Killian explained as she slipped into her lab coat. "I wanted to take a look at some old newspaper articles about August Breedlove."

"Who?"

"The head wrangler at the Bartlesville set," she explained patiently. "Remember you said you thought he'd been involved in some kind of stunt accident a few years back?"

"Oh, yes. You took time away from work to go searching for—"

"You were right, Dad," Killian interrupted, trying to stop her father from lecturing her. "A stuntman *was* killed and Gus resigned before the investigation even got underway. The stunt boss was fired on his next job for sloppy practices and was permanently suspended. The other case was closed since both he and Gus were out of the stunt association. Gus had said something about being in trouble before and this clears up—"

"Killy, we have a business to run, remember? Someday soon you'll be taking it over and you won't be able to wander off in the middle of the day."

"We should hire another partner, Dad."

"Don't need anyone else," he said, moving back into the room. "If you'll stick to this business and leave all that other stuff alone, everything will be fine."

Grabbing a clipboard holding the surgery schedule, Killian glanced at it as she joined her father. "Looks like I'll be in surgery most of the afternoon."

"What's left of the afternoon," Sam Whittier amended.

"Are we going to have this argument again?" she asked, hugging the clipboard against her chest and waiting him out.

"You'd be smart to listen to me. I built this business, didn't I? Who knows better than me how it should be run? You can't go off to Bartlesville or spend hours at the library on a wild-goose chase and expect your clients to wait for you."

"Which is why I intend to hire a partner."

"What do you need a partner for? I ran this place all by myself until you were certified. You can do it alone if you'll only keep regular hours and—"

"Dad, I'm not you. I'm proud you're planning to leave the clinic in my hands, but I'm not going to run it according to your rules and standards. I have other interests besides this clinic."

He turned his back on her. "Better scrub up."

"Dad, please don't shut me out. I want to make you understand how much I love—"

"Do the Spencers' cat first. They want to pick him up early tomorrow morning."

Killian pivoted sharply away from him and marched along the corridor to the room at the back, which was outfitted for surgery. The older her father got, the more inflexible he became, she thought as she removed the lab coat in favor of surgical green. She selected the instruments she'd need and placed them in the sterilizer as her thoughts drifted from one stubborn man to another.

Her thoughts turned to what she had read about August Breedlove. Six years ago he had been a stuntman. One of the stunts he'd been involved with had ended tragically in the death of a man named Alex Weston. Gus had resigned on the spot. Drastic action, Killian thought with a shake of her head. Just like him. She frowned, recalling how abrupt he'd been after making love to her. He'd acted as if he couldn't wait to see the last of her.

So why was she reading up on him and thinking incessantly about him? Was she a glutton for punishment? Did she enjoy having her feelings trampled upon?

It had been six weeks. Six weeks with no word from him. She'd sent him a copy of her report and the results—a stiff fine levied against the director Jerry Bishop and the suspension of Cody Turnage until he made appropriate retribution to be defined by the wrangler association. Gus had been completely cleared. In fact, his name appeared only once in the report and that was merely to identify him as Cody's boss and that he'd co-operated fully with her investigation.

Foolishly she'd thought he'd phone her to acknowl-edge that he'd received the report. But there'd been nothing.

"Nothing," she murmured, sleepwalking to the cage holding a black cat the size of a hefty raccoon. "Not one word. So, I'm not going to waste another minute think-ing about that man. Come on, Shadow," she said, lift-ing the animal from the cage. "Time to sleep. When you wake up you'll feel better. That's a promise." The cat purred and rubbed his sleek head against her hand. "If only all males were big pussycats like you," she said, laughing a little. "Life would be much simpler for us poor, foolish-hearted females."

KILLIAN SPRAYED DISINFECTANT on the stainless steel ta-ble and wiped it clean with a disposable cloth. She rolled her head around, flexing the tense muscles in her neck and shoulders.

"Six o'clock," Sam Whittier said, coming into sur-gery. "We're closed, honey."

"Good. I'm beat." She tidied up, capping bottles, cleaning the counter, switching off the glaring surgery lamp suspended above the table. "A hot bath will sure feel good tonight."

"Have you heard from Gus Breedlove since you left Bartlesville?"

"No," she said, glancing at him curiously. "I don't suppose he's too anxious to see me again."

"Why do you say that?"

"Because I'm looked upon as the enemy in camp. His nephew was the guilty party." She hitched herself up to sit on the counter and give her aching feet a rest. "He wasn't thrilled when I pointed the finger at one of his kin."

"How come you spent your lunch hour plus two more looking into his past?"

She removed one of her shoes and massaged her foot. "I've been asking myself the same question." She shrugged. "I heard him say something about having some trouble in the past and I couldn't get that out of my mind. I wanted to know what trouble."

"You don't think he mistreats animals, do you?"

"No," she answered quickly. "No, I'm sure he doesn't. He's wonderful with animals, Dad. You should see him with his horses. They love him so much. He can get them to do anything by just touching them." Remembering his touch, she slipped back in time to rumpled bedsheets and a man made for love.

"It was stupid of Breedlove to quit that way after that fella was killed. Made him look guilty as hell."

She had to think a moment before she realized her father was talking about the episode six years ago. "Yes, but I'm sure he was completely innocent."

"You are, are you?"

She removed her other shoe and dropped it to the floor. "Yes. From what I know of Gus, I don't think he'd hurt a fly."

"Is that right?"

Something in her father's tone sent a shiver of apprehension through her. "What's going on? Why are you so interested in Gus?"

"I'm not. You're the one who sounds besotted with him."

"Besotted? I am not," she denied hotly. "I swear, I can't even show a little interest in a man without you jumping to all kinds of crazy conclusions."

"A little interest? You sound more like a woman obsessed."

"Well, you're wrong."

"I don't recall you ever digging up old newspaper articles on any other man."

"Dad, let's drop it, okay?" She massaged her other foot and looked at him crossly. That's when she saw the smile lurking in his blue eyes. "Why are you teasing me about Gus when you know I'm not amused?"

"Because he's here."

She was suddenly on her feet before she realized she'd reacted. "Here? Where, here?" she demanded, smoothing her hair, leaning sideways to look past her father. "You're joshing me, right, Dad?"

Sam Whittier grinned and ran a fingertip along the short bridge of her nose. "I'm going out the back way. You lock up when you leave." He turned away from her.

"Daddy," she said, pleading, "is he or isn't he—"

"He's in the lobby waiting for you," her father said. "He's been there for over an hour, so shake a leg."

7

GUS WASN'T A COWBOY TODAY. He was a gentleman who'd come a callin' on a lady, Killian thought, taking a few moments to inspect him before he noticed her standing just outside the lobby.

No boots, nor jeans nor Western shirt this time. Today he wore dark dress slacks and a sporty plaid shirt. His thick black and silver hair looked thoroughly brushed. He studied a pamphlet on heart disease and didn't glance up until Killian stepped all the way into the lobby. Then he sprang to his feet as if he'd been ejected from the metal chair.

"Hello there," he said, sliding the pamphlet back into the display holder. "I should have called, but I thought—"

She could hardly believe that August Breedlove was standing before her again. "How are you?" she asked, needing no apology. "You look different."

"Do I?" He gave himself the once-over, making her laugh. "How so?"

"No boots, no jeans, no Stetson. But you look nice," she added, not wanting him to think for a second that she didn't find him attractive. "You're the most handsome man in the room."

He chuckled at her humor and the awkwardness of seeing her again evaporated. Relief loosened the knot in his stomach. He wondered how he had kept away from her for so long. He was glad he'd come and glad he'd stayed and waited for her.

"You've been in surgery?"

"All afternoon," she said, pulling her fingers through the sides of her straight, blond hair in an unconscious gesture. "Dad stacked them up on me and I was late getting back from lunch so . . ." Her voice trailed off and she ended in a shrug. Killian wondered if she should tell him why she'd taken a long lunch. She bowed her head to hide her private smile. "You got my report, didn't you?"

"Your report . . . oh, yes." He shifted from one foot to the other. "I thought it was fair to everyone."

"Even Cody?"

"Yes, even him. He was a damned fool and it's only right that he be treated like one."

"Gus, ease up. He's young. Maybe you expected too much of him."

"I expected only what I expect from myself—common sense, honesty and a respect for living things." He scowled, hearing the preaching tone and brushing it off. "Cody knew that, but he's a selfish kid. Maybe this will be a lesson that'll sink in. I'm glad he was suspended. I sure don't want him working around animals again."

"Me, neither. Not until he grows up."

She found herself staring at him. He looked magnificent and smelled even better. She wanted to nose the side of his neck and take a good, long sniff. She wanted to feel his arms encircle her, to feel his body warm her, to hear him tell her he'd missed her. She released a short, nervous sigh. For weeks she'd wished she hadn't gone to bed with Gus, telling herself it would be easier for her to forget him if she hadn't been so intimately involved with him. Now, however, all she could think about was being in bed with him again and how wonderful he'd make her feel. Her body tingled with sweet memories of him.

"So, tell me what's happening in your life?" she asked, trying to sound nonchalant even though she ached inside. Could she be in love with this man? she wondered. Was that why she felt out of her element, as if she'd never been alone with a man before? "Are you working on a new film?" Amazing how casual she sounded!

"No." He looked off to one side, uncomfortable with that particular subject. He didn't know if he'd ever work in films again, but he didn't want to talk about that—not with her. She'd tell him he was overreacting just as May had, and he was tired of hearing it. "I've been busy with other things. What about you?"

"Oh, you know how it is." She grimaced, aware of the lameness of the conversation. Didn't they have anything meaningful to say? "Gus, about the last time we were together . . . I probably acted as if—"

"Hey, have you eaten since lunch?" he asked, stampeding that trail of conversation. He sure as hell didn't want to discuss their lovemaking in the lobby of a veterinary clinic.

"No, I haven't."

"Let me buy you dinner."

"Well . . ." She looked down at her wrinkled trousers, blouse and thick-soled white shoes. "I'd like to change first."

"You look great to me."

She smiled her thanks. "Why don't you follow me home? Is your car outside?"

"My truck, yes."

"I don't live too far away. I'll change clothes and then—" She shook her head, changing her mind again. "What am I saying? Do you like catfish?"

"Sure. Is there a restaurant you have in mind?"

"No, but I have some fresh catfish at home. Why don't I cook some up for us?"

"I don't want you to go to so much trouble after you've been on your feet all day."

"What trouble? I was going to fry some for myself. Frying enough for two won't take any longer. You can peel the potatoes while I mix the hush puppy batter."

"Lord help me." He pressed one hand flat against his stomach. "Woman, do you know what you're doing to me? How am I supposed to be a gentleman and insist on taking you out to dinner when you're talking hush puppies and catfish to me?"

She laughed. "You're hooked, right?"

"Right. I can't turn down a meal like that."

"Let me get my purse and I'll join you outside. In case I lose you, my place is straight down this street," she said. "It's Elm Street. You go about four miles and you'll see a sign advertising the First National Bank. That sign is sitting on my land. Turn onto the road beside it and drive on up to my house."

"I think I can find it."

"Great." She dashed into her dad's office for her purse and then met Gus outside after she'd locked up. "Just follow me," she called as she climbed behind the wheel of her gold El Dorado. She drove carefully, keeping his pickup visible in her rearview mirror. Pulling onto the dirt road that led to her white-framed bungalow, it occurred to her that she'd lived in the house for eight years and this was the first time she'd have the man she wanted in it.

Gus parked his pickup behind her car. He stepped out and surveyed the area around him. Her house gave off a homey, Norman Rockwell feeling with its red roof and window boxes overflowing with red, pink and white petunias. Four dogs, ranging from shetland pony size to rat size, bounded toward him, but Killian called them off and they settled for quick sniffs of his shoes before trotting off to bigger adventures. His practiced eye sized up the parcel as being about three acres.

"How much land did you say you have here? Three, four acres?"

"Three," she said, proving him right. "I wish I had twenty or thirty more."

"You need wide, open spaces?"

"I'd like to have room to keep more livestock. For instance, Dad is looking for some acreage to put twenty head of cattle on. If I had the space, they'd be right here and my problem would be solved."

"Whose cattle?"

"Nobody's anymore. The court took them away from the rancher who starved them all winter and spring. The poor creatures . . . you should see them. They're pitiful, but they're survivors. Forty-two head have already died."

He studied her expression, sensing her sincerity, admiring her love for living things.

"How's Gold Dollar?" she asked, her gaze swinging around to his.

The reminder of that incident and the guilt he'd felt over it frayed the edges of his good mood. "Fine, considering." He knew it was a vague answer and she deserved more, but he hated talking about it. He couldn't even be around Cody without wanting to box his ears. It would be different if the kid showed remorse, but Gus could tell Cody had forgotten all about the wire he'd rigged and the damage it had done to a good horse.

"And Cody?"

He walked a little away from her and pretended not to have heard her question. If he started talking about his nephew he'd get riled and he didn't want to misdirect his anger, making her the brunt of it. "You've got a pretty place here."

"You like it?" she asked, beaming at him. "It's okay. The house is great. Big enough for all my stuff, but small enough so that it's not a pain to keep tidy. Come on in and see for yourself."

She was right about the house, Gus thought. She favored plump cushions and rocking chairs in the living room, stately, oak furniture in the dining room, white wicker with blue gingham curtains in the kitchen.

"Let me change into something else and I'll be right with you," she promised, dashing into a part of the house where he hadn't been invited. "Make yourself at home," she called to him, her voice drifting into the living room.

Gus wondered what she'd do if he strode into her bedroom and made himself home in there. He chuckled, enjoying the mental images that provoked, then he felt his desire stir to life and he shoved the imaginings aside before he made a fool of himself. Can't even think of the woman without getting hot and heavy, he scolded himself. He examined the photographs lined up on the mantel and recognized her father in several of them and a woman who must be her mother since the resemblance was so striking. Gets her looks from her mom, he thought, picking up one of the photos for a closer inspection.

"That's my mother."

He set the porcelain-framed photograph back on the mantel as his gaze swung around to her. "You inherited her good looks," he said, then his voice dried up in his throat. She'd changed into soft jeans and a white, tailored shirt she was still buttoning. His gaze followed the progress of her fingers from just between her breasts to a few inches above the shirttail. He wished desperately she'd been unbuttoning instead of buttoning.

"Thanks. I think Mother was beautiful. Her eyes were a lovely shade of blue—like Paul Newman's. Lighter than mine." She stood on one foot, then the other to pull tight the Velcro straps around the ankles of her white running shoes.

"Is your mother dead?"

"Yes," she said. "I thought I'd told you. She died fourteen years ago. Cancer." Wincing involuntarily, she waved aside the painful memory. "So, how are you at peeling potatoes, Breedlove?"

"I've skinned my share."

"Great." She crooked a finger as she pivoted toward the kitchen. "Follow me, cowboy, and I'll put you to work."

She selected the potatoes and he started peeling them while she followed her mother's recipe for hush puppy batter. The hush puppies, potatoes and meal-covered catfish were all fried outside in a huge skillet positioned above a propane-fueled cooker. Gus had never seen a woman put together a meal so quickly. In no time she had him sitting at her dining table with a feast laid out before him.

"Hope it tastes as good as it smells," she said. "I caught the fish last weekend out of my pond."

"You caught the fish?" he asked, pausing long enough to send her a questioning glance before he finished spooning home fries into his plate.

"Sure did. I love to fish."

"And I love to eat them."

"Guess we're made for each other," she quipped, and when her gaze met his, she blushed. "Hush puppy?"

"Absolutely." He concentrated on the meal, which wasn't hard to do since the food melted in his mouth. "Killian, this is about the best fish I've had in ages. You really know how to fry it up, girl."

"Daddy taught me. Most people cook it to death."

"And your mother's hush puppies are delish." He rolled his eyes and chewed, making her laugh.

"I'm glad you like the meal, and I'm glad to share it with you. I eat most of my meals alone, so it's nice to have company."

"Same here."

Killian enjoyed the food, but she enjoyed watching Gus devour it even more. He ate with gusto, sprinkling compliments about it along the way. Finding herself inordinately pleased by his flattery, she cautioned herself not to get carried away. After all, it had been six weeks of absolutely no word from him. In fact, she'd woven a scene in her head recently of how she'd snub him if she was to run into him. Now she winced, recalling how she'd almost stumbled over her own feet in her haste to see him once her father had alerted her to his presence. So much for any haughty, injured-pride act on her part.

"Why did you look me up after all this time?" she asked before she could stop herself.

He placed his napkin in his empty plate with inordinate care. "You make it sound as if it's been years since we last saw each other."

"Six weeks."

"Yes, I know." He rolled his shoulders to ease the tension that had settled there. "I didn't think you wanted to see me again. I'm still not sure."

"You think I would have invited you home for dinner if I couldn't wait to see the last of you?"

"You're a nice person and—"

"Not that nice," she cut in, losing patience. "I thought about contacting you, but that's not really my style."

"The last time we were together I got the distinct impression that you didn't want to see me again."

She stared at him, flabbergasted that he would say such a thing with a straight face. "Correct me if I'm wrong, but didn't we make love the last time we were together?"

He scowled at her sarcasm.

"I mean, that was you in bed with me, right? Not your evil twin?"

"Look, just because two people make love doesn't mean they're joined for life."

"Ah, so it was you," she said, stacking dishes to keep her hands busy; otherwise, she felt she might hit him. "After what you just said I'm certain it was you."

"What?"

"That making love with me didn't mean that much to you."

"Hey, wait a second." He grabbed her wrist before she could charge into the kitchen, plates in hand. "That's not fair. You kissed me off first."

"When?" she challenged.

"I don't know...you said something about it being the end for us."

"Oh, *pleeeze!*" She jerked her wrist from his grasp. "I said nothing of the sort. You just wanted me out of your way once the good part was over."

"Bull!" He catapulted from the chair, furious. "I made it clear from the beginning that I wanted you."

"Right, and you had me." She angled her chin up in a show of pride. "And I didn't hear a peep from you for six weeks. What was I supposed to think? I sent you my report, clearing your name, and nothing. Not a line in the mail or a phone call. Nothing."

"Like I said, I didn't think you wanted to hear from me."

"You think I sleep with every cowboy that swaggers my way?"

"No." He ran a hand down his face in abject frustration. "No, I don't think that. Never did. Not about you."

Examining every nuance of his expressive face, she satisfied her instincts before giving a tense nod. "I believe you." She backed off, her anger diminishing. "Anyway, I'm glad you finally came around."

"So am I." He picked up the glasses and a couple of bowls and carried them into the kitchen for her. "I thought about you a lot."

"Did you?"

"Sure did."

"That's nice."

He could tell by the tone of her voice, she wasn't listening to him. Just replying, but not completely believing or comprehending. She leaned down to place the bowls and plates in the dishwasher. Gus moved to stand behind her for a better view of her heart-shaped rear. Still bent over, she looked back at him, then straightened and spun around.

"Hey, what are you doing back there, grinning like a wolf on the prowl?"

"Nice description," he murmured, remembering the smell of her perfume and the way it scented her whole body. "That's exactly how I feel."

She shook her head, making her hair swing like a golden curtain above her shoulders. "No, Gus. Not tonight." She pointed to the back door. "Why don't you prowl outside while I finish loading the dishwasher? There are some comfy chairs out on the patio. Go on, and I'll join you in a jiffy."

"Sending me away, are you?" He reached out one hand and ran the back of his fingers along her warm cheek. "I have been thinking about you and those thoughts never fail to arouse me."

"Gus, don't . . ."

"Mostly I think about the things I wish I'd done. Wish we'd taken a shower together, or better yet, a bath."

"Gus, come on . . ." She laughed and it was a nervous, high-strung breath of sound.

"Wish we'd lolled in bed and told each other secret things—secret desires and dreams and what turns us on and off. Lovers should do that. We should have done it and then we wouldn't have spent six hellish weeks wondering if you were wondering about me or if I was wondering about you."

He gave her the opportunity to point him outside again, but she didn't, so he stepped closer, erasing the distance between them. He ran his hands lightly up and down her arms, resisting the urge to crush her to him and kiss her until she begged for mercy.

"Do you have secrets, Gus?" she asked. "Do you have confidences to share with me?"

"I have lots of things to share with you. You know what else?" he whispered, skimming his lips across her forehead. "I wish I'd spent more time exploring . . . the small of your back, behind your knees, the undersides of your breasts. Those soft, tender places a woman shares so seldom. A man can get lost in those places." He looked into her eyes, half-lidded and splintery blue. "I want to get lost in you, Killian. Just like before."

Then he kissed her and she kissed him back. Soft, yearning kisses that plucked at his lips and left them moist and throbbing. His hands drifted over her breasts and around her waist to pull her against him. Her body felt boneless, like clay ready to mold to the contours of his, and it did, touching him in places that pulsated, pounded, pleaded for more.

That's when the blessed voice of reason arrowed into his numb mind and told him not to ruin a good thing. He listened reluctantly and set her from him. Her smile told him he'd done right by her.

"Meet you outside," he said, and somehow he found the will to actually turn and stroll out under the stars.

He gobbled clean air into his lungs, flinging back his head and expanding his chest until he felt the buttons on his shirt strain. Lord, that woman went to his head like wine, he thought. He decided he'd rushed things before, sweeping her off her feet and taking her in a whirl of hot passion. Next time—if there was to be one—he wanted to take it slower. He wanted to court her, lead up to a night of loving that would result in a morning of lingering laughter instead of quick getaways. Next time they'd look each other in the eyes the morning after instead of ducking and running.

An awning stretched over the brick patio, shielding the furniture and two cookers, one charcoal and one fueled by propane. Beside them stood two bags of charcoal— one nearly empty, the other unopened—and a canister of propane gas. He smiled, glad to see that she liked to cook out. So did he. Steaks, ground beef, pork, fish, it all tasted better grilled. Pots of red geraniums sat here and there. Airy ferns and airplane plants swung from shell and macramé hangers. Nothing like the touch of a woman, he thought, impressed with her green thumb.

Sitting on the squeaky glider, he focused on lowering his body temperature. The rest of the evening would be spent in polite conversation, he counseled himself. No caresses or kisses that grow hotter and hotter . . .

He groaned, aroused by the images racing like wildfire through his mind. Looking up at the stars, he listened to the clatter of dinnerware being loaded into the dishwasher and he counted the seconds until she'd be with him again.

A cold nose lifted his hand off his knee and Gus opened his eyes to find that he'd been joined by a black cocker spaniel. He stroked the dog's sleek head. Another dog, this one a mutt of questionable parentage, stood back and waited for an invitation.

"Come here, baby," Gus said, snapping his fingers and then holding out his hand to the shy one. "I won't bite if you won't."

The newcomer edged closer, but as the dog drew even with the charcoal bags, the empty one fell over, blown by a breeze that came skipping across the patio. Startled, the dog yelped, tucked its tail and ran halfway across the yard before it stopped and looked back at Gus and the bewildered cocker. Gus laughed, tickled by the skittish dog and the trick that had been played on him by the breeze.

"Coward," he called. "You silly—"

The back door slapped open and Killian stumbled through with the look of an avenging angel on her face. She looked at the shivering dog and then her blazing eyes fastened on Gus.

"What did you do to him?" she demanded in a tone that made Gus want to let loose with some choice words. "Is he hurt?"

Gus pointed to the sack that had fallen over. "The breeze toppled it and that dog of yours is a mite nervous." He listened to her words again in his head, hearing the accusation and not liking it one bit. "I didn't touch him. I did pet this one," he said, nodding at the cocker. "But, as you can see, he's still in one piece. No visible scars. No blood."

Her shoulders sagged. "Gus, please. I didn't mean—"

"Yeah, well, I've got to go," he said, slicing into her lie before she could voice it. He knew the truth and no simpering half-truth or apology could vanquish it. She didn't trust him around her animals. Her report might have cleared him, but he was guilty in her mind. "Thanks for dinner."

"You're not leaving like this, are you? I'm sorry if I—"

"Don't," he said, turning toward her long enough to send her a quelling glare. "Don't apologize for your gut instinct."

"You don't understand. I rescued that dog from a man who—"

"Mistreated it?"

"Yes," she said, moving toward him. "And I'm overly sensitive about—"

"I understand. Really." He shook off her pleading expression. "I'm glad we saw each other again, Killian. Goodbye." He strode to his pickup, anger churning in his gut.

Killian watched him leave, helpless to stop him. Whirling, she kicked the charcoal sack, wishing it were her own rear. "Why did you do that to him?" she said as tears rolled down her cheeks. She'd done some dumb things in her life, but tonight she'd won the blue ribbon for stupidity.

8

DIALING THE TELEPHONE NUMBER, Killian wondered for the umpteenth time whether or not she was doing the right thing. After last night, she'd fretted about how she could make amends to Gus and had finally come to this—a plea in lieu of an olive branch. Now all she had to do was convince him she was sincere so that he'd accept her peace offering. The connection went through and the phone clicked, ringing in Gus's house. Killian closed her eyes, imagining his home. She saw him in a ranch-style house with big rooms and leather furniture. She could see him striding toward the phone—across glossy, hardwood floors—boot heels sounding like cannon fire in the quiet room.

"Hello?" Gus said, picking up the receiver while he held a towel wrapped around his hips.

His voice made Killian's eyes pop open, and for a few scary moments, she couldn't muster a sound.

"Hello," he repeated, impatiently, squeezing the receiver between the side of his face and his shoulder.

"Good morning, Gus," she said, finding her voice. She looked at the clock set inside an old iron skillet hanging above her kitchen stove. Just after eight, she thought, wishing she'd checked the time before she'd called. "Sorry if I'm disturbing you. I know it's early and—"

He looked down at the prints his wet feet made on the carpeting and glanced at the mantel clock. Eight. Of all mornings to sleep in . . . her fault . . . he'd been so furious with her he hadn't been able to sleep until after three or four in the morning. "I've been up for hours," he lied, shifting uncomfortably as water drops trickled down his legs and slipped from his soppy hair to his wet shoulders.

"Oh, good. I was afraid I might have gotten you out of bed." She squeezed her eyes shut against the mental image that conjured up.

"I'm wide awake." He rubbed sleep from his eyes with his free hand.

"Right, well, I enjoyed your visit yesterday . . . until the end. That misunderstanding was so unfortunate." She plucked a napkin from its holder on the table and began shredding it.

"Forget it." He ran a hand through his hair and flung droplets off his fingertips.

"I will if you will." She held her breath, waiting, knowing he wasn't about to actually forget the incident. Would he lie to her or squirm out of an answer?

"Can you hold on for a sec?"

"Sure."

"Thanks." He put the receiver down long enough to towel off and grab his robe off a hook in his bedroom closet. "I'm back."

"We were talking about last night," she reminded him, unwilling to let him forget.

"Do you want something? I'm kind of in a rush." He juggled the receiver on his shoulder while he overlapped the sides of the robe and tied the belt at his waist.

Killian finished destroying the napkin. "Okay, fine. I'll get down to business. Remember those cattle I told you about?"

"Not really."

"The ones starved by their owner. They need a home, someone to care for them."

"Oh, right." He made a face, wondering what they had to do with him.

"I want you to take them."

"Where to?"

She gathered up the napkin confetti. "Your place. Can I bring them to you tomorrow? Will you take them?"

"You mean until you find a permanent place for them?"

"No," she said, drawing out the word. "I'd like to leave them in your hands. After you fatten them up, you could sell them off, I suppose."

What a squirrelly idea, he thought. "Killian, I'm a horseman, not a cowpuncher."

"I know, but this is a special case. The cattle are at the stockyards and they're not doing too well there. I've got to move them. They need special attention—more nutrients than they can get at the stockyards. I'll be glad to donate my medical services if you want."

"I'd like to help, but—"

"I'd keep them myself, but I haven't the room. You do."

"Yes, but—"

"I can't think of anyone I'd rather leave them with. Gus, they're so pitiful. They've been through so much, the poor creatures. Can't you work your magic on them, Gus? Please, do it for me. They'll be dead within a week if I have to leave them at the stockyards." She realized she'd risen from the chair, galvanized by her urgent plea. She could hear him breathing and wondered if she'd swayed him to her side.

"Oh, hell. Bring them on." He realized he'd dropped onto the bed, weakened by her pleading voice.

"Thanks, Gus," she crooned into the phone. "You're such a dear man."

"No, I'm not."

"You are. I knew I could count on you."

"Yeah, well . . ." He felt stupid, shy, gosh-gee-willikers glad she thought he was dear.

"I'll bring them out in the morning. Is that okay?"

"Sure. I'll be looking for you."

"Thanks again, Gus."

"Hey. . ."

"Yes?" She listened intently, sensing he was hesitant.

He scowled at his reflection in the bureau mirror, re-calling the implied accusation last night and how it had sliced through him like a machete. "Are you sure about this? I mean, are you sure you want to leave them with me?"

She took a moment to place steel in her voice. "I'm positive you're the right man." Then she hung up, deter-mined to have the last word.

IT WAS ACTUALLY AFTERNOON by the time she drove be-hind the two cattle trailers onto Gus's land. White rail fences spoke of horse country, making Killian more aware of how gutsy she'd been to ask Gus to take the cattle and how good-hearted he was to accept them. She parked her car near the house while the trailers pulled up alongside the stables and exercise yard.

The house wasn't ranch-style; in fact, it was almost a twin of hers. It had a black roof instead of a red one and it might be a room larger than hers. No wonder he'd made himself at home at her place so quickly, she thought.

"I'll find out where to unload them," Killian shouted to the two men who had graciously agreed to drive the cattle from the stockyards to the Breedlove ranch. Then she went to look for Gus.

Since no one answered when she rang the doorbell, she went to the stables. One of the hands there sent her to the big, red barn. Inside, it was shadowy with spears of sunlight shooting through cracks and crevices. Nothing stirred except dust motes.

"Gus?" she whispered, then tried a stronger voice. "Gus?"

"I'm here." His voice came from above.

"Where?" Killian searched the loft, then heard rustling and footsteps. Gus appeared at the edge of the loft, near the ladder. That's when Killian noticed his blue-plaid shirt hanging over one of the rungs. Her gaze traveled up again. She could see all of him now. Bare-chested, his skin glistened with sweat. His jeans were tight, worn threadbare at the knees, and over the fly. Her gaze followed the thin line of black hair running down his stomach to where it disappeared into the beltless waistband.

"You're late. I thought you'd be here early this morning."

"I know," she said, as if speaking by rote. "It took longer than I expected." She moistened her dry lips with the tip of her tongue, then pulled at the front of her blouse. "Whew! It's warm in here," she said, watching his hand slide down his damp chest to his flat stomach. *And getting hotter*, she thought.

"It's warm everywhere. We could use some rain."

"We're supposed to get some this weekend," she said. Is this it? she wondered. Had they been reduced to discussing the weather?

"I was checking on the kittens."

She grabbed at that conversational lifeline. "There are kittens up there?"

He nodded, glancing over his shoulder into the part of the loft hidden from her view. "Eight of them. Their mama gave birth last week."

"May I see?"

"Shouldn't we tend to the cattle?"

"Yes, I guess so." She knew he was the kind of man who would attend to his duty first and foremost. "I borrowed a couple of stockyard men to drive the trailers here. Where do you want the cattle unloaded?"

"How bad are they?" he asked, looking down at her from above.

"Pretty bad. They worsened last night. We lost one of them."

"Hmm." He drummed his fingers against his chest. "I was going to put them out to pasture, but I better pen them up and feed them grain for a few days. Let them out into that barbwire fenced corral behind this barn."

He turned his back to climb down the ladder. Killian enjoyed the view. Nice butt, she thought. Tight, muscled, compact. Good legs. Long, lean, powerful. Great back. Smooth-skinned, copper-colored, rippling with muscle. He skipped the last four rungs, dropping onto the balls of his feet like a big cat. He retrieved his shirt, but didn't put it on. He used it as a towel, rubbing it over his damp chest, under his arms, down his neck.

"Need me to help?" he asked, when she stood rooted to the spot.

"No, they can manage." She forced herself to turn away from him and walk briskly to the trailers. No sound came from within, dramatizing the weakened state of the cattle. They were too frail to even moo. She could see through the slats that most of them were lying down, unable to stand during the trip. The sight of them, the silence of them, chased away any lingering thoughts of Gus. She peered inside one of the trailers and whispered encouragement to the miserable creatures.

"Where to?" one of the drivers asked.

"Behind the barn. There's a pen there," she said, pointing the way. "I'll meet you over there."

She went to the barn to oversee the unloading. The drivers were patient, herding the cattle from the trailers, coaxing them to stand, gently prodding them down the ramp and into the pen. The cattle stood in their new home, heads down, legs quivering, eyes gummy with poor health. Two lay down, exhausted.

"Thanks, guys," Killian said to the men. "I owe you."

One waved off her gratitude. "Glad to help. Poor, dumb animals. Awful to treat them bad when they can't do a damn thing to protect themselves. At least we're quick at the stockyards."

She nodded, agreeing. The slaughterhouse was far more humane than this slow, agonizing death. The men went back to the trailers and drove off.

"Godalmighty."

The softly spoken word spun Killian around to see Gus striding toward the pen. He'd put his shirt on. The tails flapped as he walked toward her, his gaze sweeping over the pathetic-looking herd in the pen.

"They look like death."

"They nearly are dead, Gus."

"I've never taken care of animals this malnourished," he said, rubbing his forehead with one hand as if he suddenly had a migraine. "If I'd known they were this bad off, I wouldn't have let you bring them here. I'm not equipped to handle—"

"Yes, you are. They need food. They need shelter. They need someone to watch over them. You're equipped."

"I don't know," he said, opening the gate and going inside. "I hope whoever did this is in jail."

"He was, but only for thirty days. He was fined, too. I'm trying to get the government to stiffen the laws about mistreating domestics." She had more to say, but she curbed her tongue, knowing she had a tendency to launch into a lecture. She'd worked so hard and so long for animal rights, she had to constantly remind herself not to come on like gangbusters every time someone unwittingly gave her a cue.

Gus examined each new ward in his own way. Watching him, Killian knew she'd made the right decision in bringing them here, even though his was a horse ranch and cattle weren't his interest. He stroked their heads, ran his hands over their bony sides, massaged their trembling limbs, examined the sores on their bodies, and all the while spoke in a soothing whisper.

"Hey, little girl," he whispered to one. "Easy, baby. This old cowboy's not going to hurt you, girl. Bless your hide, honey. You've been through the torture mill, haven't you? Poor baby. Poor starved darlin'."

Sweet emotion tightened Killian's throat and stung her eyes. She bowed her head, thankful she'd found a man like Gus and resolved to make things good between them. This was a start. Bringing the cattle to him had been her way of showing him that she trusted him: it negated her behavior the other night when she'd spoken without thinking of the consequences. He'd demonstrated that he wasn't about to listen to a reasonable explanation, so she'd had to find another way to make him understand that she really never thought he'd hurt her dog or, for that matter, any other living thing.

"One or two of these look as if they might not make it to morning."

"Yes, I know," Killian said, her gaze moving to the two in question. "Do your best, Gus. That's all I ask." She decided to bring up last night again while she had him penned up. "That dog last night—the one that yelped. I've only had him a few days. A man brought him to the clinic and said he'd found him walking down the middle of Main Street. He's so skittish, so afraid every time there's a quick movement or a sharp word, that it doesn't take a genius to see he's been kicked around all his life. When I heard him cry out, I charged without thinking first. If I'd given myself half a second to think, I would have asked you calmly what startled the dog instead of making it sound as if I thought you'd drop-kicked him."

Since his back was to her, she couldn't tell if she'd pleased him or infuriated him.

"Well, are you going to tell me to take a flying leap through a rolling doughnut or tell me I'm forgiven and that you still like me a little?" she demanded, clutching the top of one of the fence posts for support.

"That's why you brought the cattle here, right?" he asked, twisting around to look at her with hooded eyes.

"I brought them here because I had my back against the wall. They were dying at the stockyards. I didn't save them just to let them drop like flies. You were the only one I could think of who would give them the care they needed." She stared back at him when his expression hardened. Finally, she relented. "And I thought it would be a swell way to let you know that I trust you. If you'd been a nice man and accepted my apology the other night, then you wouldn't have a herd of sickly cattle on your hands today."

His grin was slow and delicious. His chuckle warmed every corner of her heart. "I hadn't thought of it that way. First time I've ever been punished for not forgiving someone for being a jerk."

She winced at his description, but decided not to challenge it. "You'll have to hand-feed some of them," she said, switching her thoughts back to the debilitated cattle. "If there are any too weak to chew, I'll come out and feed them intravenously."

He rubbed the back of his neck. "Sounds like I've got my work cut out for me."

"It'll be worth it just to see them get stronger and stronger every day."

"I guess."

She laughed at his unenthusiastic response. "Well, I've delivered them, so I suppose I should go and let you—"

"Do you have to run off?" he asked, turning to face her. When she arched her eyebrows and smiled, he glanced at the toes of his boots. "I mean, what's the hurry? I thought you could stick around for a spell and give me some pointers on how to treat these animals. I haven't been around cattle in a long time. Of course, I understand if you have to get back to the clinic."

"It's Saturday. We close at noon on Saturdays," she said, glad he wanted her company. She certainly wanted his. "I guess I can stay awhile." She clasped her hands around the post, leaned back and swung from side to side. "Does this mean I'm forgiven?"

He eased around the cattle and came toward her to rest one hand on top of the post. "You're forgiven," he said, swaying closer so that she could see the glint in his earthy brown eyes. "And I like you—a little."

"A little, huh?" she asked, liking the teasing tone in his voice and responding to it.

"I'll like you more after you help me mix some feed for these animals and help me haul some water in here for them."

She groaned. He laughed. Killian felt as if a weight had been lifted from her heart. It soared again.

BY LATE AFTERNOON the cattle had been fed and watered. Killian had written out a diet for the malnourished animals, designed to provide a powerhouse of vitamins and other nutrients in measured doses. The cattle could only eat and digest small portions. Three of them refused to eat, and Killian and Gus had hand-fed them with a funnel.

A marvel of patience and perseverance, Gus had followed her orders to the letter. Killian demonstrated to two of his ranch hands how to mix the food and funnel it into the cows' stomachs. They'd help Gus with the six daily feedings required until the cattle were able to feed on their own.

It had sprinkled off and on all afternoon, cooling and light, not enough to hinder the work. By late afternoon a bank of clouds had mounted in the sky, swirling and churning, with bursts of thunder and streaks of lightning.

"You're going to get rained on, mister," Killian called to Gus, cupping her hands around her mouth. She'd given Gus a tube of ointment for the cattle's sores and he was determined to apply it to those in need before he called it a day.

"Hope so. I've been wanting a good, soaking rain for weeks," he answered, not looking up from the task at hand. "I'm sure these cows wouldn't mind, either."

Booming thunder sounded overhead. The stronger cattle moved into a knot in one corner of the corral. Gus eyed the threatening sky.

"Guess we should go in before it rains buckets," he said, capping the tube of medicine and putting it away.

"I should be going, but I was wondering if you'd let me see the kittens in the hayloft."

"Sure, but wouldn't you like to stay—" Another clap of thunder stole his words, then the clouds opened up and rain fell in hard, drenching sheets. He flung his arms wide open and turned his face up to the rain. "Finally!" he shouted. "I was beginning to think I'd have to name this place Dry Gulch."

"I'm getting soaked to the skin," Killian said, jumping off the fence and dashing to the nearest shelter, the barn. She lost time looking for a back entrance, and finding none, had to scamper around to the front.

Once inside she slung her wet hair back from her face, then propped her hands on her knees and leaned over to catch her breath. She was still breathless when Gus barreled in, his shirt clinging to his body and his hair plastered to his head. He laughed, and gasped for air. Standing in front of her, hip-cocked, his dark eyes glinting, his smile dazzling, he was about as irresistible as men come, and Killian's breath was stolen again—not to mention a few other senses, as well.

That wayward, wanton thought brought her upright. She laughed, heard the trembling uncertainty of it, and told herself to get a grip. Just when she thought she'd regained her equilibrium, he unbuttoned his shirt and peeled it off. Killian surged toward the loft ladder, desperate to put some distance between her cravings and his body.

"I'll go up here and see the kittens, then I'm out of here," she said, already climbing the ladder like a scared monkey. *What are you frightened of, silly?* she questioned herself. *He's not a stranger. You've been to bed with the man, so why are you acting as if he's some dark marauder and you're the only virgin in the county?*

The cloying sweetness of hay drifted into her nostrils as she climbed into the loft. Dust motes drifted in the hazy light. Her shoes made rustling sounds as she moved slowly, her eyes tracking the unfamiliar territory. She heard mewling and then a cat peeked over a mound of straw.

"Hey, there," Killian whispered, dropping onto all fours to creep forward the rest of the way.

The cat purred, sounding unnaturally loud in the quiet of the loft, and blinked green eyes, startling against her black-and-white face.

"May I see your babies? I can hear them. Are they frightened of the thunder?" Killian gained ground and rose up to look over the protective wall of straw. Eight balls of fur suckled the mother cat—four black, two black-and-white and two pure white. "Oh, they're so pretty," Killian said, inching a tad closer to stroke the mother's head. "You're just as proud as a peacock over them, aren't you? Don't fret. I'm not going to bother them."

"Since this is her first litter, she's squeamish about anyone messing with her babies," Gus said, having climbed the ladder behind her.

Killian nodded, sitting back on her heels. "She's a young cat."

"Just over a year old. After this litter is weaned, I'm having her spayed."

"That's a good idea. Cats are prolific."

"They sure are. When I bought this place, it was over-run with them. Never saw so many hungry cats. I bet there were at least fifty running wild around here. I moved the horses in and the cats left, except for three or four brave ones. Her mama was one of them."

"She's a pretty thing."

"She sure enough is." His voice had changed from impersonal to very personal, indeed. A purr of satisfaction ran through it and awareness of him coiled in Killian's stomach.

Killian stroked the cat again before moving back and then rising to her feet. She turned slowly toward Gus, letting her lashes sweep up over his tight, threadbare jeans to his lean waist and wide chest. He held his shirt in one hand. With a flick of his wrist, he discarded it. The action embodied danger, decision and desire.

"Damn, if you don't look like you did the first time I saw you. Remember that rainy night?"

"Yes. I'll always remember." She stared at the center of his chest, somehow unable to look at his face. Dark, swirling hair grew between his flat, masculine nipples. She knew how that hair felt—silky, springy, sexy.

"Look at you," he murmured, his voice growing scratchy. "I can see your nipples through your shirt." He grinned. "Are you cold or just glad to see me?"

She jumped, looked down at the small peaks poking through her white bra and blouse, and crossed her arms over them. His laugh sent her gaze to his.

"I've seen them before," he reminded her, unnecessarily. "I've touched them. Had them in my mouth."

"I know," she said, suddenly tense. Was he laughing at her? Making her squirm for his own amusement? "I was there, too."

He smiled and there was something predatory in the gleam of his teeth and the sparkle in the depths of his caramel-colored eyes. "Take off your blouse and stay awhile," he said, that purr bordering on a growl as the pussycat changed into a tiger.

She tried to sound flippant. "In a hayloft? How trite."

"When was the last time you rolled in the hay with a man?"

"This would be the first," she said, hitching up her chin. "But I think I'll skip the experience. As I said before, I need to be getting home. It'll be dark soon—"

"I can't let you leave without a roll in the hay. Just wouldn't be right."

"—and I've overstayed my welcome," she finished just to spite him. She glared at him, damning his grin, despising him for taking lightly what weighted her every dream, her every fantasy. "Sex *means* something to me, Gus. A roll in the hay holds no appeal to me, whatsoever."

He shifted, squaring his shoulders. "What's got your back up?"

"I'm not one of your damned cats," she spat, then tried to dart past him to the ladder, but he was as quick as a mouse and caught her wrist. "Let go. The rain sounds as if it has let up and I—"

His mouth stopped her words. She managed a garbled sound of protest that went unnoticed. He hooked one hand at the back of her neck and pulled her off balance so that she fell against him. She was certain steam rose off their bodies upon contact. In fact, she would have sworn she heard a sizzle. She felt it—felt the heat rise off him and seep into her to warm her blood and make her simmering sexuality bubble—boil.

He wrapped the fingers of his other hand in her tangled hair and pulled her head back until her eyes almost touched his.

"Sex means something to me, too," he said between clenched teeth. "The trouble with you is you take it too seriously. It's not all work. It's supposed to be fun, Killian."

Her temper sparked. It was a powerful sensation, being aroused and angry at the same time. She didn't know if she was getting more turned on or more incensed. "The trouble with you is you lose all your charm once you're satisfied. You all but pushed me out the front door. I'm surprised you gave me time to dress."

"I wasn't pushing, you were making fast tracks out the door without any help from me."

"If I was, it was because I didn't enjoy being treated like a hired bimbo who didn't know the meter had stopped running."

"That's a crock. You're the one who was talking end-ings and goodbyes."

"You didn't correct me."

"No." He took a long breath and his eyes lost some of their flashing anger. "I learned a long time ago that you can't hold somebody who doesn't want to be held."

"I wanted to be," she said. "I hated you for practically shoving me out the door. I hated you, but there wasn't a day that went by that I didn't want you again." She re-leased a shivery sigh. "Fools suffer gladly."

"No more," he said, angling her head back, looking into her eyes as if she were the only woman on earth. "No more, by God, no more."

His kiss melted her bones. She dropped to her knees in the hay, then wilted onto her side. He pulled her blouse taut over her shoulders and the top button popped off. The others slipped free of the buttonholes, one by one. She dragged her arms from the sleeves, turning the blouse inside out before she was done with it. The bra was less trouble and then the pleasure was all hers as his mouth closed over one of her breasts and then the other. He tongued her, making her nipples taut. Killian stroked his smooth, damp shoulders and wet her hands in his rain-slicked hair. She held his face and felt his cheeks hollow as his tongue surged into her mouth. He nibbled her lips, traced their shape with the tip of his tongue, then traced a line of moisture down the column of her throat to her breasts.

Nuzzling the undersides of her breasts, he unfastened her jeans and tugged them off her hips and legs. She kicked them aside and raised her rump enough for him to slide off her panties. His jeans felt rough against her skin and the metal snaps were cold and unwelcome.

She inched her fingertips under his waistband and drew down the front zipper slowly, the sound personifying sex. The top snap caused no problem. Killian slid her hand inside. Gus winced as she freed him. He rose up on his knees and pushed down his jeans, never taking his eyes from her face, she never taking hers from the bold beauty of his maleness.

When he was about to enter her, he stopped and raised himself up on his arms. She curled her fingers into his supple buttocks, urging him to complete what he'd started, then she saw a hint of a smile on his mouth.

"Are you sure a roll in the hay holds absolutely no interest to you, whatsoever?" he asked.

She groaned her impatience and locked her heels at the small of his back. "Nobody likes a tease, Gus." Laughing, she lightly clasped his neck and lifted herself up to meet his open mouth. She felt the tip of him touch the fire in her.

"Maybe we should wait and go inside . . ."

"Gus," she said, moaning. "Your control is not amusing."

"No, I mean, I don't have anything with me. Protection."

"Don't worry." She kissed him hard and fast. "I'm okay."

"Thank heavens," he breathed.

She smiled, realizing he was aching for her. And then he drove inside her and she melted around him. She clung to him, giving herself over to his rapid pace, matching him gasp for gasp. Emotion seared and burned away everything except the power of him and the firestorms his mouth touched off. He played with her nipples and she cried out for mercy. Her body shuddered with longing and her mind screamed for a release from the passion that had built to an impossibly high peak.

Killian opened her eyes just enough to see his face. His eyes were tightly shut. Beads of perspiration mixed with the raindrops slipping from his hair onto his forehead and cheeks. Then his hips surged and his pelvis bucked against her. The clinging scent of sex overtook the musty smell of hay. The strange perfume added eroticism to an already charged atmosphere.

Something wild and wonderful burst within her and she dug her fingers deeply into Gus's buttocks. Thunder stampeded across the sky, drowning out their cries of pleasure.

Gus wilted against her and whispered her name as if it were part of a prayer. Killian smiled, too weak to respond. Only their ragged breathing accompanied the patter of rain. Killian shivered, suddenly cold. She reached for her clothing and laughed when Gus tried to keep them from her. Finally, she managed to wriggle out from under him and bound to her feet.

"Where do you think you're going?" he asked, snatching up her blouse. He stood and held it up in the air, out of her reach. "If you think you're going home, then you're wrong, lady."

"I'm going to get dressed enough to make a decent run from here to the house," she explained, jumping up and snagging the blouse with one hand. "Then I'm going to jump into a hot shower and warm up. Does that meet with your approval, sir?"

"How about a bath, instead?" he suggested, his voice taking on that sexy growl again.

"How about both? One can never be too clean," she teased. "And there are good points about both showers and baths."

"Especially when *you're* in them," he tacked on. He grabbed his jeans and stepped into them. "Race you," he challenged.

"You're on," Killian called, already heading for the ladder. Gus was hot on her heels.

9

"THAT WAS QUITE an experience," Killian said to Gus, who was sitting at the opposite end of the big, claw-footed tub. Candlelight played over his face, throwing shadows over it.

"What was?" he asked, his tone telling her he was barely listening. He was too engrossed in massaging her left foot. She rubbed his chest with her other one, slipping her toes through the slick, salt-and-pepper hair that spread across his broad chest and then arrowed past his navel.

"Making love in the hayloft," she said dreamily. She tipped her head back, resting it on the rim of the tub. He's the most magnificent lover, she thought, but kept it to herself. No sense in giving him a big head, she decided with a smile.

"Taking a roll in the hay, you mean," he said, a grin nudging the corners of his mouth.

She blew a sigh at the ceiling. "Why do men have to say such crass things?" She punched him in the stomach with her heel. "However you put it, it was memorable. But I suppose it's old hat to you . . . rolling in the hay, taking a bath with a woman, giving her an allover body massage."

"Sure," he agreed. "I do it every day." He grinned when her heel punched him again. "It's my moonlighting job. I usually charge a grand for such services, but since you're special, I'll only charge you a hundred."

"Fat chance," she murmured, eyes still closed.

"You remember that film...gigolo...*American Gigolo*. That's me. I'm the Oklahoma Gigolo."

She laughed at that, raising her head enough to peer at him through her lashes; then she widened her eyes for a better look when it struck her how much he resembled the actor in that film. She'd never noticed before...even his body reminded her of a scene in that film. Resting her head on the rim of the tub again, she closed her eyes and played the scene in her head, substituting Gus for the actor, making for a particularly provocative fantasy.

"Maybe I'll just charge you fifty bucks. I've enjoyed this more than I usually do with my other clients."

"Gee, thanks."

"Okay, okay. It's on the house."

"Big of you," she said, then opened her eyes to slits. His gaze wandered from her feet to her face, taking its own, sweet time. "Why doesn't a great-looking guy like you have a devoted gal? I'm amazed by my good luck. It's not every day a woman finds an unmarried man as gorgeous as you."

He chuckled, never ceasing his gentle manipulations of her foot. The pad of his thumb made lazy circles across her instep and his long fingers stroked the top of her foot.

"Quit being the strong silent type," she complained. "Talk to me. I want to know things about you."

"You ought to already know everything there is to know about me. You investigated me, remember?"

"I learned a little about your work as a film wrangler. I want to know about you, the man. Why don't you have a woman in your life?"

"I thought I did."

She smiled, liking the sound of that. "Besides this woman. Who was my predecessor?"

"You are without peers."

"August Breedlove, out with it!" She pulled her foot from his grasp and sat up, unmindful of her nudity, comfortable with his. "Tell me about yourself."

"Let's talk about you."

"Oh, Gus." She fell back, making the water slosh.

"I hear that clinic of yours is busy."

"It is, but it's not all mine. I co-own it with my father. He's supposed to retire next year and then I'll take over."

"You'll run it by yourself?"

"That's what my father wants." She fished the washcloth and soap from the water and worked up some suds.

"From the way you said that, it doesn't sound as if you and your dad see eye to eye." His voice echoed in the tiled bathroom. It seemed to envelop her, wrap her in its rich timbre.

"We don't. I'm going to hire a junior partner to help me with the clinic and Dad is fit to be tied over it. He expects me to operate the clinic just as he did before I received my degree and joined him. He thinks anything short of total dedication is a slap in his face." She hooked her feet under his knees and pulled herself close to him, then she ran the sudsy cloth over his face, caressing the bridge of his nose and the ridge of his cheekbones. He closed his eyes, contented. "Daddy can't understand why I have outside interests."

"What outside interests? Anyone I know?"

"Not that kind of outside interests," she said, rubbing his lips with the cloth. "I was talking about my work with the humane societies. I'd love to have a spread like this so that I could take in some of the maltreated animals I've come across. Daddy expects me to give up my outside work once he retires, but I'm not going to do it." She rinsed the cloth, wet it thoroughly, then held it just above his face and squeezed. Scented water dribbled over his cheeks and chin, chasing away the suds. "But Daddy keeps arguing, fussing, fuming. He makes me feel that I must run the clinic his way or I'm an ingrate."

"Sounds like he doesn't want to retire."

"No, he does. He's got big plans. He bought a motor home and he's going to travel. He's always wanted to see the country. The clinic has tied him down."

"And now he wants it to tie you down."

"Exactly." She snuggled closer, slipping her arms around him and kissing the curve of his neck. "I knew you'd see it my way."

"You do want the clinic, don't you?"

"Yes, I do, but I don't want to be owned by it like my father has been ever since I can remember." She shut her eyes as he embraced her. His arms were strong but gentle, and his hands seemed to take the stress from her body. She hadn't been so relaxed in months. In fact, she hadn't realized how stressed her life had been lately until Gus had massaged her taut muscles. "When Mother died he took off the day of the funeral and then went back to work the very next day." She shook her head adamantly. "I'm not made that way. I need time to heal. I need time for myself."

"Do you love your father?"

"I'm crazy about him." She lifted her head from Gus's shoulder and found understanding in his eyes. "I don't want you to think that I don't worship the ground he walks on, because I do. I'm just not going to live my life according to his rules any longer. That upsets him, but I can't help it. Maybe I am an ingrate."

"No, you're a woman with a mind of her own." His hands fanned across her back. "A beautiful woman with a mind of her own. Hey, what about you? Who was my predecessor?"

"For the life of me, I can't recall his name." She laughed against his lips, then enjoyed his slow, wet kisses. She took up the washcloth again and wiped off the remainder of soap from his nose and chin, then ran it across his shoulder and arm. She'd bathed every part of his body— twice. They'd taken a shower together before filling the tub for a long soak. Suddenly, she wanted him to know how special the day had been for her. It was important that he understand he was in a class by himself. "Can I tell you something . . . something serious?"

He cocked one eyebrow. "You're not an ax murderess, are you? I mean, it's nothing like that, is it?"

"No, silly." She linked her arms loosely around his neck. "I want you to understand something about me."

"I'm listening."

She gathered in a big breath, then let it out along with a jumble of heartfelt words. "Gus, I've never felt this . . . this comfortable with any other man." She lowered her gaze, suddenly shy. "I've never done this kind of thing before . . . never trusted so completely that I could bare my body and my soul. But it feels good . . . it feels right. It's a relief to let myself go and not be afraid of making a fool of myself." She framed his face in her hands. "You've set something free inside of me."

He pulled her to sit in his lap. The touch of his mouth on her breasts acted as a tonic on her, conquering her secret fear that she might live her life alone, assuaging her hidden anxiety that she might never love a man enough to want to bear his children. She wanted everything from him and more. But was the feeling mutual? Did he trust her as fully as she trusted him? she wondered. He hadn't talked to her about the trouble he'd had during his stunt days. Why not?

"Gus, what did you do before you were a movie wrangler?" She arched up, giving him more access to her tingling breasts. She combed her fingers through his wet hair, admiring the frosting of silver among the inky strands. His hair was short, but showed no hint of thinning.

Throw open the gate and let me in, she begged silently. *Tell me about the accident. Trust me as I trust you.*

He moved her so that her back was against the tub and stretched out against the length of her. "You want to talk about that now?"

"Why not?"

"Because I can think of a hundred better things to do in a bathtub than talk about jobs we've had." He slipped his hands under her hips and lifted her up to meet his thrusting body.

"Gus!" She braced herself, gripping his shoulders, watching the dark passion leap into his eyes. "You don't play fair," she whispered huskily as he delved deeper inside her. His kisses lulled her, seduced her. Soft, wet kisses that stirred her soul.

"I play to win," he rasped. "And I'm out to win you."

"You haven't been listening," she said. "You've already won me."

Outside it was still raining, beating a tattoo on the windowpanes. Gus sprinkled kisses over her throat. His eyes became heavy-lidded, his mouth more sensuous with each stroking kiss. His tongue was tipped with fire, lighting her inside and out. The heel of his hand moved down her stomach to the triangle of golden hair and began an erotic massage.

She sought his mouth with hers and exchanged frenzied kisses. Then his body surged against hers, sloshing water over the sides of the tub. The delicious tension built and then exploded inside her.

Much later they realized the water had cooled and they were shivering. Killian raced him to the bedroom and snuggled under the sheet with him.

SHE AWOKE WITH A START, surprised she'd dozed off, then wondering how long she'd been asleep. Killian sat up, gathering the sheet close to her cool body.

"Gus?" she called, still drowsy.

No answer. The imprint of his head on the pillow assured her this was no dream. Killian exchanged the sheet for Gus's shirt. She put it on and buttoned it while she went from room to room searching for him. She stood in the living room and rubbed sleep from her eyes. She yawned and looked around for her shoes and clothes that had been thrown hither and yon when she and Gus had left the hayloft and raced each other to the shower. The memory made her smile and want him next to her.

"Well, since this is his home, he has to come back sooner or later," she said, feeling deserted and chiding herself for giving in to that feeling. The clock on the mantel struck four. It was dark outside, moonless and cloudy. She thought of the cattle and wondered how they'd fared during the rainstorm. She pulled on her damp jeans and tennis shoes, then went out the back door.

The clean smell of rain hung in the air and a moist breeze billowed Gus's shirt, making her realize how large it was on her. Its hem fluttered to her knees. Jumping puddles, she ran to the barn and to the pen behind it. The sight of Gus wandering among the cattle brought her to a halt. She covered her mouth with one hand, suppressing her delighted giggles.

We're so much alike, she thought, watching him move from one heifer to the next, running his hands over their heads, backs and bony sides.

Gus, lost in thought, examined each cow. Several head gathered at the feed trough and chomped noisily. He murmured encouragement, glad they were feeding again. None were down—another encouraging sign. Maybe they'll make it, he thought. He hadn't given them much hope earlier, but he could see they'd turned the corner. Of course, it would take months before they'd be up to snuff. By this time next year, they should be fat and sassy, he surmised, looking forward to that day.

Look at yourself, he thought, chuckling under his breath. A horseman worried about a bunch of puny cattle. That gal has turned your life upside down, he told himself, and you're loving every minute of it. Once the newness of their coupling had worn off, would Killian stick around? He'd been burned a couple of times by women who were here today and gone tomorrow and he was tired of that shallow kind of encounter. Once, he'd valued his reputation as a solitary horseman, but not any more. Killian had made him long for a partner—a partner for life. He'd wanted that once before and it had slipped through his fingers like grains of sand.

He should tell Killian about that other time, he thought. She'd asked him, but it was hard for him to talk about it. He'd buried it deep inside so it wouldn't destroy him. Sooner or later, she'd find out. He stared up at the cloudy night sky, wondering if she'd accept his side of the story or if he'd see doubt enter her eyes again. God, he couldn't take it if she started questioning his honor again. What if she thought he was a coward . . . what if she thought he was a fool for turning his back instead of standing his ground . . . what if—

"Is it possible I've found someone as goofy about animals as I am?"

Gus whipped his head around at the sound of her voice and his heart liquified and surged into his throat. She had his shirt on. Simple, but so erotic. The sight of his shirt on her curvy body made him want to thrust his hands up under the fluttering hem and fill them with her creamy breasts. She had the prettiest breasts. Rosy, soft, sweet-tasting breasts.

She propped her hands at her hips. "Well? You going to answer me or stare me down?"

He cleared his throat before trying his voice. "You didn't have to come out here. I just wanted to check on them. I was afraid the weak ones might be down in the mud."

"But they're all on their feet," she said, moving gingerly across the muddy ground. She stopped at the fence, peering over the top row of barbwire. "It's a miracle. You certainly have a way with animals, Mr. Breedlove."

"Don't go thinking I've done something special. I do believe the rain revived them." He went from one to the other again, checking them with his hands, feeling his gut wrench when he saw fear in their rolling eyes. "Why did that man starve them like this?"

"He said he didn't have the money to feed himself, much less them."

"So why didn't he sell them?"

"Said he couldn't find a buyer."

"Bull. He just didn't give a damn."

"You're probably right."

"Somebody ought to pen him up and starve him."

"I think they're going to make it. Thanks, Gus. I owe you one."

"No, you don't." He made his way toward her. "I'm glad to help out. Besides, you set out to prove you trusted

me around animals, and you did it. I appreciate the vote
of confidence." He pulled off his rawhide gloves and
tucked them into his back pocket. "You look mighty cute
in my shirt." Bending over, he ducked between the lines
of barbwire, then straightened to take her into his arms.
He fulfilled his fantasy, sliding his hands up under the
shirt to cup her breasts. She swayed forward, her lips
parting, inviting his tongue.

Her lips were cool, but the inside of her mouth was
wonderfully warm. He explored it with his tongue, slipping it back and forth until he couldn't stand it anymore. He broke away and gasped for breath.

"Can you die from wanting someone too much?" he
asked, resting his forehead against hers.

She laughed and tightened her arms around his neck.
He lifted her up. Her feet dangled an inch above the
ground. Her blue eyes looked enormous, her lips thoroughly kissed. She smelled of soap and fresh linen and
rainwater.

"Come back inside with me," he whispered. "I'm going
to make love to you until dawn."

"I love your eyes." She kissed his eyelids, then stroked
his eyebrows with her gentling lips. "So dark, so deep,
so warm. I'm a sucker for brown eyes."

"What about the rest of me?"

"The rest of you?" She smiled as he began walking toward the house, carrying her along with him. "There's
something to be said for the strong silent type."

"Is that me? Strong and silent?"

"You're not an easy man to know, August Breedlove.
You make a woman work at it."

"Do I? I thought I was an easy lay."

She frowned. "I'm not talking about that. I'm talking about what's inside you. What makes you tick? What makes Gus run?"

He stopped just in front of the back door, stunned by her phrasing. Did she know that he had a history of running or was that just a lucky guess?

"What's wrong?" she asked, worry clouding her beryl-blue eyes.

"Nothing." He shook his head, pushing back his urge to confess. There would be time for that later, but now he only wanted to bury himself inside her again where it was warm and secure and oh, so close to heaven. He set her on her feet long enough to open the back door, then he scooped her into his arms and took her straight to bed.

POPPING THE LAST BITE of biscuit and gravy into her mouth, Killian looked across the table at Gus and patted her stomach.

"Mmm, mmm, good," she said, complimenting him on a scrumptious breakfast. "You're a good cook, good in bed, gorgeous out of it and great with animals. Is there anything you don't do well?"

"No," he said, propping his chin in one hand. "I'm perfect."

"That's what I was afraid of," she said with a belabored sigh. "There's nothing more boring than perfection."

"I spoke too quickly. I snore and I've been known to sulk when I don't get my way."

"Ah, good. I love a man with imperfections." She indicated the dirty dishes. "Shall I wash or dry?"

"You just sit there and look sexy. I'll take care of these." He stood up, then went to the sink to peer out the window. "We've got company."

"Who?"

"Cody and May." He glanced at her. "I forgot that I invited them for Sunday breakfast."

Killian stood up as the back door swung open and May and Cody entered the kitchen.

"Hey, sis," Gus greeted his sister, and shook Cody's hand. "You remember Killian Whittier, don't you, Cody?"

"Sure. Hard to forget her," Cody said, recovering nicely as he shook Killian's hand. "Good to see you again."

"Hello, Cody." Killian held out her hand to his mother. "We haven't met, but I've heard a lot about you. I'm Killian Whittier."

"May Turnage," the other woman said, shaking Killian's hand. "Glad to meet you. I've heard a lot about you, too."

Yes, I bet you have, Killian thought, then stepped back, feeling like the odd man out.

"You've already had your breakfast?" May asked, looking at the evidence on the kitchen table.

"Yes, we couldn't wait. We were starved." Gus grinned and winked at May. "Killian brought some poor, mistreated cattle over and we worked up an appetite tending to them. You don't mind, do you? I've still got biscuit dough, and gravy only takes a minute to make. How many eggs y'all want?" He hustled to the stove and tied on an apron. "Y'all want sausage, bacon or ham?"

"I'll take three eggs and ham," Cody said, straddling a chair. "Got any coffee made?"

"I'll pour you some," Killian offered, then held out a chair for May. "Sit down, please. I'm sorry we didn't wait for you." She felt like a conspirator, falling in with Gus's version of things. He's quick on his feet, she thought, impressed with the way he'd told the truth without actually saying that Killian had spent the night with him.

"It's okay," May assured her, sitting in the chair. "Gus, one egg will do me, and ham sounds good. You making milk gravy or red-eye?"

"Red-eye," he replied.

"My favorite," Cody said, helping stack dishes and hand them to Killian. "What's this about cattle? You changing over to cattle ranching, Uncle Gus?"

"No, I'm taking them as a favor to Killian."

"They were starved. I needed to find a place for them to recuperate, and Gus graciously took them in," Killian explained.

"Starved?" May asked. "Ain't that awful. Some people need to be strung up by their thumbs until they either attract flies or some sense."

"Are you investigating their owner?" Cody asked.

"No." Killian turned her back to stack the dishes in the sink, hoping Cody wouldn't place her in the position of chief interrogator again. She didn't want to dredge up the disappointments of the past. "Your uncle is a good cook. I can't remember the last time I had homemade biscuits," she said, changing the subject.

"He's a wonder," May agreed. "Cooks better than me, that's for sure."

"That's because he likes it and you hate it," Cody said. "Mom has never been fond of the cook stove."

"Look who's talking," May said. "I don't see you spending time in the kitchen, either. If it wasn't for bologna and sardines, you'd starve. Do you like to cook, Killian?"

"Yes, but I'm not as good at it as Gus. I take shortcuts. Canned biscuits, microwave recipes, that sort of thing."

"She cooks out a lot," Gus joined in. "Don't be fooled, May. This gal can whip up a mean meal. I told you about that catfish she fried for me."

May nodded. "Your hush puppies are now legendary."

"They are?" Killian swung her gaze around to Gus, but he kept his eyes glued to the frying eggs and ham.

"Sit down, Killian," May said, patting the chair beside her. "We'll clean up after everyone's eaten."

She was left with no choice but to join Cody and May at the table. Looking from one to the other, she wondered if they resented her. After all, she had sent Cody to the unemployment line and that couldn't have pleased his mother.

"How have you been, Cody?" Killian asked when nothing else came to mind.

"Great," he said, surprising her with his cheery response. "How have you been? Working on another movie?"

"No. I hardly ever do that. I've only worked three film sets."

"And you got your man every single time, I bet," Cody said, a thread of resentment running through his voice.

"Here, Cody, fill your mouth with these." Gus set a plate of eggs in front of his nephew. "Ham's coming."

"Thanks, Uncle Gus." He gave Gus a half smirk, half smile, then attacked his eggs.

"May, you like yours scrambled, right?"

"Any old way, Gus. Don't go to any trouble."

"May, scrambled or not?" Gus repeated with a twinge of impatience.

"Scrambled." May made a face at his back, and Killian laughed. "He's a grouch in the morning, isn't he? No wonder he lives alone." Her gaze wandered knowingly over Killian's wrinkled clothes and bare feet. "You ever been married?"

"Me?" Killian gulped, startled by the question. "No."

"Gus, neither. He's been roped, but not tied." She poured milk into her coffee and stirred it slowly, thoughtfully. Killian had the distinct impression that May had put two and two together and figured out that Gus had left out some of the story about the nature of Killian's visit.

Gus handed May a plate of scrambled eggs and ham, then refilled the coffee cups before he pulled the biscuits from the oven. He set a bowl of red-eye gravy on the table and a tin of browned biscuits.

"So, tell me," May said, helping herself to a biscuit. "Should Cody and I start shopping for a wedding present?"

10

STUNNED INTO SILENCE, Killian looked to Gus to dig her out of answering May's question but Gus had lost his voice, too. His lips moved but nothing came out.

"Come on, Ma," Cody said, riding to the rescue. "Just because two people spend time together doesn't mean they're talking mortgages and disposable diapers."

"I should hope not," Gus said, recovering. "No child of mine would wear a disposable diaper anyway. Those things are a blight on the environment."

"I agree," Killian said, falling in line. "I approve of diaper services."

"What about good old-fashioned washing and then drying them on an outside line?" May asked.

"No problem as long as the husband shares in the washing and drying," Killian said, glancing at Gus and getting a grin of admiration from him. "Most men wouldn't agree to that, I'm afraid."

"This one would," Gus said, then cleared his throat and adjusted his manner. "How's the food? I cured that ham myself."

"Is this one of the Christmas hams?" May asked.

"Yes, but I've got three more, so don't worry. We'll have plenty come Christmas."

"It's mouth-watering," May said, finishing off her second slice. "Everything was. I'm helping with the dishes." She held up her hands to stop the protests. "No, I am, so save your breath. Then me and Cody are leaving to give you two lovebirds some privacy."

"May, give it a rest," Gus said, sending his sister a dark look, then switching his attention to Cody. "What have you been up to lately, partner?"

"Not much." Cody hooked his thumbs through his belt loops and leaned back, lifting the chair's front legs off the floor. "I've been helping Ma out some around the place."

May's sharp glance at Cody made it clear that he'd just told a big fib. Killian shifted uneasily, sensing the friction. Suddenly, the atmosphere was charged, dangerous.

"You know you might be reinstated in the wrangler association if you take their classes again and keep your nose clean for a year," Gus said, drumming five fingers on the tabletop. "They're willing to give you a chance."

"I know, but that's two years out of my life," Cody said. "I've already given them a big enough chunk of me."

Feeling as if she should offer encouragement, Killian looked from Gus's dark scowl to Cody's foolish smirk. "Cody, I'm sure the association will be lenient since it was your first offense. They know that Jerry Bishop is the real culprit."

"She's right," Gus said, fingers still tapping. "If you won't listen to me, listen to her."

"I'm listening," Cody said, his words slowed by boredom. "But I'm not interested in wrangling anymore."

"What *are* you interested in?" Gus asked, sitting up straight and crossing his arms on the table. "Besides lying in bed on your lazy butt and living off your mother's good intentions."

Cody's eyes sparked with anger and his jawline tensed as he gritted his teeth. "Not that it's any of your business, Uncle Gus, but I'm thinking of going to Nevada to work in a casino with a friend of mine."

Gus hissed through his teeth. "Don't tell me. I'll bet this friend is a female firecracker."

"What if she is?" The chair legs hit the floor with a bang. "Like I said, it's none of your—"

"Business," Gus finished for him. "But it *is* my business if it reflects on me. Your antics sure as hell reflected on me last time, didn't they? I knew you had about as much common sense as a two-year-old, but I never figured you for a quitter, Cody."

A hateful cast fell over Cody's face. "I learned from a master, I reckon. Like you, I'd rather duck and run than face the music. Hell, why hang around a bunch of do-gooders—" his gaze touched briefly on Killian "—who think I'm a criminal? I'd rather hop on a fast horse and make tracks for a friendlier place. Just like you did, Uncle Gus."

"I don't have to take that kind of talk from you," Gus said, shooting an arm across the table to point belligerently at his nephew. "I diapered your bare butt and I—"

"Hey, hey, guys," Killian said, feeling more sorry for May than Gus or Cody. Caught in the middle, May looked from one man she loved to the other, unsure of which side to take or whether to even take one. "Let's all simmer down," Killian suggested, trying to laugh them out of their surly moods. "This happens in the best of families, but I think you two should stop hurtling insults before this gets completely out of hand."

Gus swung around to Killian and the blaze in his eyes singed her. "This is *family* business, and you're out of line."

"Gus, I—I—"

He sliced through Killian's stammering shock with a chopping gesture, then hitched his head toward the door. "Cody, let's take this outside. It's time we cleared the air."

"Fine." Cody shot up, sending the chair skittering backward, and marched out the back door.

"Gus, please don't," May said, clutching her brother's shirttail before he could follow her son.

"We won't come to blows," Gus said, easing away from May. "I just want to talk to him. Don't worry." Then he was gone, leaving May and Killian to exchange worried glances.

"Gus means well. He's been like a father to Cody, but Cody's full grown now and doesn't want his uncle's advice. Gus is having trouble handling that."

Killian nodded, thinking of her own complications with her father. "It's hard to let go."

"For some people, I guess." May shrugged, then stood up and began clearing the table. "As for me, I'll be glad when Cody takes off on his own. I raised him and now it's time for him to leave the nest and make his own way. I told him yesterday that he's welcome to come back any time for a visit, but I don't want him coming home to live every time he hits a rut in life." She paused in her work.

"Do you think I'm mean to tell him that? You think a mother should be unselfish?"

Killian reached out to clasp one of May's work-roughened hands. "I think the best mother knows when to assert her independence. Children should always feel they can go home again, but they should make their own homes as well. That's what being an adult is all about."

"It sure is," May agreed. Her carefree laughter lightened the atmosphere. "You going to help me with these dishes?"

"I sure am. That's what women do while their menfolk talk, right?"

"That's what they did in my mama's house, but I kind of changed the rules when I set up my own homestead."

"How long were you married?"

"Four years. Not nearly long enough. Sometimes I can't even remember what married felt like." She carried a load of dishes to the counter and then began filling the sink with hot water, adding a dollop of liquid soap.

"You never remarried?"

"No. Cody kept me busy enough." She laughed again, her laughter going up and down the scale. "I'm glad I just had one child. Two would have killed me. Cody would have done me in if Gus hadn't been around to help out. He's going to make a fine father some day." May cut her eyes toward Killian. "And a fine husband to some lucky lady."

Killian set the dirty dishes next to the others on the counter, then wagged a finger at May. "You're incorrigible. I can see where Cody gets his ornery streak and his knack for speaking his mind, and the consequences be damned."

"Well, I got my faults," May said, becoming somber as she began washing the dishes and setting them in the drainer for Killian to dry with a soft dish towel. "Gus shouldn't have bit your head off when you tried to settle him down."

"He didn't mean it," Killian said, but she still felt the sting of his words. "He was very upset."

"Cody shouldn't have brought up the past."

"The past is hard to outdistance," Killian said, eyeing the other woman, wondering if May might reveal something to her about Gus, hoping she would.

"Don't I know it." She sighed wearily, then began vigorously scrubbing a skillet. "Can you believe that Cody? Going to Nevada to work in a casino. That new gal he's been sporting with has convinced him there's a pot full of money waiting for them in Vegas. Cody will believe anything if it's attached to money or a buxom blonde." Her gaze strayed to Killian's bustline.

"Don't worry. I'm blond, but not exactly buxom," Killian said, then doubled over with laughter while May turned beet-red before giving in to a bout of giggles.

"I didn't mean to insult . . ." May waved aside her attempted apology, and was seized by laughter again. After a few moments she recovered enough to add, "After I said it, I realized you were blond and . . . oh, never mind. You know I was funning."

"I know." Killian looped an arm around May's narrow shoulders and gave her a squeeze. "Maybe Las Vegas is just the place for Cody. They're both flashy and full of fun. I feel bad that he's not going to try to make amends with the wrangler association. Wrangling's a good job for a young man."

May nodded, returning to the dishes in the sink. "I was real pleased when Gus talked Cody into going to the classes. I never thought Cody would stick with it, but he did. Guess he was romanced by the glamour of the film business. He probably thought he'd jump from wrangler to movie star in no time at all."

"If only he hadn't listened to Jerry Bishop. May, I was only doing my job when I—"

"I know, I know," May said consolingly. "I don't put any blame on you. Cody was brought up better than to hurt some poor horse, especially one raised and trained by his own uncle." She frowned as she rinsed the last of the dishes. Squeezing water from the sponge, she went to the stove and wiped it clean. "What hurts so bad is that he stirred up painful memories for Gus." She looked over her shoulder at Killian. "How's he holding up? Is he in good spirits?"

"I think so."

"Gus worries too much about what people think of him. He's always been concerned about his reputation. He wants people to trust him, think of him as a man of his word. That's how Daddy raised us. Daddy used to tell us that a good reputation was better than money in the bank. Of course, things have changed since Daddy's day. Honor and a man's word don't count for as much now, but they do count with Gus."

"I've noticed," Killian said, hopping up to sit on the counter. "But Gus has a good name in the wrangler business."

"He thinks it's tarnished now. He thinks people are doubting him again like when he did stunts. He's always regretted not standing up to those people. He should have stood his ground and made them prove their insinuations." May pitched the sponge into the sink in a moment of anger.

"Why didn't he? It seems out of character for him to walk away from a controversy."

"He wouldn't have turned his back on it if his heart hadn't gotten in the way." May leaned a hip against the stove and stared into space, her thoughts taking her away from the kitchen and Killian's company.

"His heart?" Killian asked, bringing May back to the present. "What do you mean? How was his heart involved?"

May blinked away her inner musings. "Well, you know he was . . . you know about . . . Gus has talked to you about his stunt days, hasn't he?"

"Some," Killian hedged, but she could see that May was unconvinced. "The stunt coordinator was the one eventually charged with negligence, wasn't he?"

"That's right." May went toward the back door and looked through the pane of glass in it. "Wonder where those two went. Me and Cody ought to be getting home."

"Why did Gus walk away from the investigation of that accident? He certainly didn't walk away from my investigation."

"Learned his lesson, I guess," May said, still looking out the window.

"But you said something about his heart . . . was he personally involved somehow with—"

"You should ask Gus," May said, turning to face Killian. "It's his life and he should be the one to tell you what happened. Not me. I'm not going to say anything else about it." She turned her back to Killian and stared out the back door.

Killian nodded. She knew when she'd been dismissed. Besides, May was right. Gus was the one to explain. And he would, she thought. Before she'd leave here today, he would.

CODY SHOVED HIS HANDS into his jeans pockets and stared sullenly at the cattle.

"They sure are poorly," he said, glancing at Gus. "Reckon you'll lose some."

"Hope not." Gus squinted sideways at his nephew and judged that tempers had cooled down enough to talk. "Now, what's this about Vegas? Boy, you know that's a place for suckers."

"I don't know nothing about it because I haven't been there and I'm no boy."

Gus sighed. So much for reasoning with him, he thought, studying Cody's hard-line expression. "Well, I have been there and it's a place to lose your money. And I know you're not a boy, but old habits die hard and you've been under my wing for many a year."

"But not lately."

"No, not lately," Gus agreed. "Cody, will you listen to me one last time and forget this scheme about Vegas? Your gal is wrong if she said you could make big money there. You've got to have big money to make big money. You can't believe those stories of folks plunking down five bucks and leaving the table with five hundred thousand. That happens once in a blue moon, and you've never been lucky."

"Maybe my luck's changing. Besides, my girl has been there and she did real well for herself."

"Oh, yeah? Then why did she leave?"

"Because her mama got sick and she came home to see to her. That okay with you?" Cody asked, his glance full of resentment. "You haven't even met her and you already think she's a shiftless liar. Or is it a reflection on me that you think every female interested in me is low-class and out to bamboozle me?" He held up a hand when Gus opened his mouth to speak. "Look, why don't you get off my back?" His face reddened with anger. "I don't need you or Ma telling me what to do. I'm growed."

"Me and your ma want the best for you, Cody. Why can't you stick with something solid? What's wrong with helping your ma around the place? She's broken her back raising you and you thank her by being so lazy, dead lice won't even fall off you."

Cody's lips pulled away from his teeth in a snarl. "Get this straight. I ain't you. And what's more, I don't wanna be. Ma wants that spread, not me. I got my own plans. Why is it so hard for you and her to get that through your heads? I'm my own man with my own way of thinking. Busting my rear on some piece of played-out land isn't my idea of living, okay?" He folded his arms and turned his back to Gus. "If I never see another cow, it'll be too soon. That's all I'm saying about it. I ain't fighting you no more, Uncle Gus. I'm leaving here and I was hoping to leave on good terms."

Gus mirrored Cody's posture as defeat weighted his shoulders. "You know, Cody, you and me are good at hurting each other. That's our problem. You know I'm touchy about my stunt days, and I know you don't like being told what to do. I had hoped we'd find some way to work with each other, either as film wranglers or on this land. Guess I was dreaming, huh?"

"Guess so. You wanted me to follow in your footsteps, but I want to make tracks all my own. Even if they're shallow tracks that lead nowhere, at least they'll be all mine."

They were quiet for a spell, both of them watching the cattle shuffle along the hay-strewn ground. Finally, Cody propped one boot on the lowest rail and looked over his shoulder at Gus.

"I shouldn't have done it."

Gus didn't have to ask; he knew Cody was talking about trip-wiring the horse. What he didn't know was how relieved he'd be once the apology was finally offered. Some of the weight lifted off his shoulders and he felt a smile tug at one corner of his mouth.

"That's right. You shouldn't have. You knew better."

"Yeah," Cody agreed with a long sigh. "I sure enough did. The money was tempting, but I knew it was wrong to go for it. That director made it sound as though I was doing everybody a big favor, and I admit it was what I wanted to hear. But in my heart, I always knew I was selling you out. You'd taught me good, Uncle Gus. You and Ma. One thing you should understand is that your teachings have made me know the difference between right and wrong. Once that horse was hurt, I felt like a big old cow biscuit. I couldn't look anyone in the eyes for days."

"I noticed," Gus said, thinking back. "But I didn't want to believe that you could hurt an animal and then just leave it for somebody else to doctor."

"I figured as much. That made me feel even worse."

"What?"

"That you believed in me so much. That you were defending me all over the place." He picked a splinter of wood off the fence. "You've got mighty high expectations about everyone, Uncle Gus."

"Is that wrong?"

Cody shrugged. "The higher they are, the farther you got to fall."

"That's a hell of an attitude."

"It's a hell of a world." Cody slipped his boot off the rail and looked squarely at Gus. "Ma is okay about me going to Nevada. She knows I'm not happy hanging around here."

Gus started to offer another bit of advice, but he choked it back down his throat. Instead, he held out his hand. "Good luck, then."

Cody's smile was bright with relief and he shook Gus's hand vigorously. "Thanks, Uncle Gus." Then he pulled Gus close for a quick hug. "You're not so bad."

"Gee, thanks," Gus said with a touch of sarcasm, but he appreciated the hug more than Cody would ever know. Heartfelt admissions were scarce between them, always had been. Gus thought about mentioning that, but he stopped himself. Cody didn't want any sentimental talk. He just wanted to get, now that the getting was good. "I'm glad to get your seal of approval."

Cody laughed, then glanced in the direction of the house. "Better get. Ma'll be pawing the ground by now."

"Is she pretty—this gal you're going to Vegas with?" Gus asked.

"She's not as good-looking as Killian, but she's no slouch," Cody said, falling in step with Gus when he started for the house. "Ma sure would like it if you'd get hitched."

Gus chuckled. "Well, if I do, it won't be to please May."

"You thinking of getting married?" Cody asked, clearly amazed.

"It's crossed my mind." He cuffed Cody's shoulder playfully. "Let's keep that between me and you for now, okay, partner?"

"You got it. You can trust me."

Gus bit his tongue and smiled. No use ruining a truce, he told himself. No use telling Cody he trusted him about as far as he could throw him. Nope. Not even that far, he amended.

May came outside, clearly worried. When she saw that neither was bruised or bleeding, she flashed a quick smile. "There you are. We're finished with the dishes. Ready to head home, Cody? I got horses to feed and exercise."

"I'm ready." Cody stuck his head inside the kitchen to wave at Killian. "See you around, hon."

"See you, Cody," Killian said, turning from the sink she'd been scouring. "Good luck in Nevada."

"Thanks." He winked slyly. "And good luck to you. Lord knows you'll need it if you're looking to woo old Gloomy Gus."

She laughed, shaking her head at his impertinence. Funny, but she didn't think of Gus as gloomy. Intense, yes. Intense, moody, a bit mysterious, but a man who loved life and all it offered. Not gloomy at all. Of course, Cody had a different perspective. He saw Gus as an uptight older man who had sown his wild oats and had forgotten how much fun it had been.

"Good to meet you," May said, stepping inside to get her purse and truck keys. "I hope I see you again real soon."

"Me, too." Killian went to the door, watching Gus send off his sister and nephew. When May and Cody were gone, she opened the back door and went to stand beside Gus in the driveway. "I like your sister."

"She likes you, too." He smoothed the wrinkles from the front of his shirt. "Guess I owe you an apology."

"Guess so." Killian clasped her hands behind her back and waited.

"I was out of line."

"That's it? That's the apology?"

He made a face at her. "You want me to beg your forgiveness? I thought you'd be gracious about this."

"Okay. I accept your apology. I understand that you were mad at Cody and just lashed out at me because I got in your way."

"That's about the size of it. I'm glad you explained it to me."

She nudged him with her shoulder. "May thinks the world of you."

"I hope so. I'm her brother."

"It's more than that. We had a talk and it was obvious you're someone she looks up to."

"That's good." He stared into the far distance. "Want to wander over to the cattle pen? Maybe we could find some hay to roll around in."

"Later." She stepped around to face him. One thing she didn't want to do was get sidetracked by his intoxicating kisses. Not yet, anyway. "Gus, what's eating at you?" Resting her hands on his arms, she tried to will the truth from him with her eyes. When that didn't work, she resorted to the direct approach. "Can't you trust me enough to tell me?"

"It's nothing. Cody just knows the right buttons to push to send me into orbit. I swear, that kid will end up behind bars if he's not careful. Of course, he did apologize for trip-wiring that horse. That's something, I guess. Remorse is a start to developing a conscience." He puffed out a sigh. "I had such high hopes for him. He was a good kid up until he discovered girls, then his integrity and good sense headed south while the rest of him went north."

"It's not just Cody," Killian insisted, refusing to let him brush her off again. "After last night, I thought you'd share things with me. I want more than a fun weekend from you, Gus. Am I wrong to want more?"

"No." He dropped his head for a moment as if seeking some guidance from within. "I'm thinking of quitting the wrangler business."

"Don't kid around," she said, then felt her mouth drop open when she saw he was serious. "You can stand there and say that after calling your own nephew a quitter?"

"I was sticking around for him. I thought if he wanted to come back, I'd stay in the association to support his decision and be a good example for him, but Cody's not interested and—"

"Forget Cody, what about you?" Killian asked, grabbing handfuls of his shirtsleeves and giving him a shake. "You haven't done anything wrong, so why are you cashing in your future?"

"I know this business and the people in it better than you do. I know there are producers—big-name producers—who don't want lawsuits or allegations. My name might spell trouble in the industry." He held up his hands when she started to argue, then brought them down sharply to wrench his sleeves from her grasp. "I didn't say I was definitely going to quit. I'm just thinking about it. A man can change his career gears, you know. It's not like I'm folding up my tent and disappearing into the night."

"Gus, why would you chuck all your wrangler work just because someone who worked for you got greedy? It's stupid."

"If you knew the whole story, you wouldn't be so quick to call me that."

"So, tell me." She stepped away from him. "Tell me the whole story."

"Let's drop it."

"No!" She stood her ground, blocking his escape. "I want to hear your story. I want to understand why you're thinking of running."

"Who said anything about running?"

"Sounds like it to me. Sounds as though Jerry Bishop got his scapegoat, after all. Not just one, but two. Cody *and* you. Bishop gets a black eye and you two turn tail and run. How charming."

His face hardened. "I don't have to explain myself to you."

Disappointment loosened her tongue. "No, you don't, and I don't have to wrestle with a closed book when there are plenty of others on the shelf." When he refused to yield, she selected a sharper sword. "Cody was right. You're the kingpin of quitters." She marched into the house.

"Where are you going?" he called after her.

"Home." She stormed through his house, picking up her belongings, searching for her car keys, her purse.

"Don't dash off just because I'm not in the mood to—"

"I'm tired of your moods," she shot back. "If I wanted to mess with them, I'd buy a mood ring and watch my own fluctuate."

"A what? You're not making sense."

"And you are?"

"I'm not the one running now."

"I'm not running. I'm escaping." She saw the corner of her purse sticking out from under the couch and went down on all fours to drag it from its hiding place. "Come here, you. Always hiding when I need to make a grand exit."

"You're talking to your purse now?" Gus asked, executing a couple of side steps to block her, then resorting to brute strength to keep her from leaving. He grabbed her upper arms and bent his knees so that he could be at eye level with her. It was like looking into the eye of a hurricane. Fury blasted from her to him and shook the truth loose. "I had some trouble before, when I was a stuntman, Killian. Someone was killed in a stunt I helped plan, stage and execute."

His confession decreased her fury by half. "You're going to talk to me now? You're going to stop with the moody blues act and tell me what's been bothering you...what's been eating at you ever since you found out I was going to investigate your wranglers?"

He straightened slowly, loath to dredge it all up, but resigned to her pigheadedness. "Yes, if that's what it takes to keep you from running off like a woman scorned. Hell, yes! Let's talk about it. I'll tell my sob story and then you'll be happy because I *shared* with you." He ran a hand through his hair. "I don't know what good it will do, but if it'll make you happy, fine." He pivoted and dropped to the couch like a stone, glaring at her with a baleful expression that made her look away in discomfort.

She flung her purse and jacket into a nearby chair. "Why is this such a chore for you, Gus? Is it so terrible

that I want to know about your pain, your disappointments, your troubles? I told you about mine and it felt
good to have you understand, to console, to advise."

"What troubles?"

"With my father," she said, exasperated. "And how he
wants me to run things his way and how we fight about
it constantly."

"Oh." He flapped a hand, letting it fall heavily back
onto his knee. "Paltry stuff, darlin', compared to my lot
in life. I'm glad I helped ease the burden, but my burden
is considerably more hefty."

She sat on the floor in front of him, crossing her legs
and leaning back on her arms. She knew the story, but
she wanted his version and she wanted him to fill in the
blanks. What distressed her was that he couldn't understand why it was so important to her that she know.
Didn't he realize she'd fallen in love with him, that his
worries worried her, that his troubles troubled her? *For
better or for worse, Gus,* she thought. *Please lean on me
so that I can, in turn, lean on you.*

He propped an elbow on the arm of the couch, then
set his chin in the palm of his hand. He stared off to the
side at nothing, but Killian knew something was brew-
ing in his gut, festering in his soul.

"Tell me. Do this for us," she whispered. "If not for
you, then for me. I need to know, Gus. I can't keep poking around, hoping to strike a nerve. I feel as if I can tell
you anything, and it hurts me so to think that it's not
mutual. It hurts that you're holding back from me...that
you don't trust me with your deepest feelings." She
reached out to him, leaning far enough to touch his

denimed knee. "What happened back then? You don't really feel responsible, do you?"

"You don't think I should?" His gaze swung to her and his eyes were glassy. "For all you know, I *am* responsible. I told you it was my stunt."

"I know a little about it," she confessed. "I spent a few hours in the library reading old newspaper clippings."

"Figured you did."

She looked down at her interlocked fingers. "But I wanted your version of what happened."

"Alex Weston died in a stunt I conceived." He rubbed his face with his hands until his skin stung. Yesterdays crowded into his head and some of those old feelings of helplessness, despair and grief penetrated his armor like arrows. "It should have gone off without a hitch and it would have if the stunt boss hadn't been in such an all-fired hurry that it go off on time. The director was on his case because the shooting was falling behind schedule." His laughter felt harsh against his throat. "Same old thing, huh?"

Killian nodded, exchanging bitter smiles with him. She lifted her knees and looped her arms around them. "Some directors would give away their children if they saw it as a way to save time." She deepened her voice to an authoritative roar, "Time is money!"

"And we're running out of both," Gus finished. "I've heard that more times than I can count."

"That's why there are people like us around film sets, Gus. We are the voices of reason."

His eyebrows lifted and fell as her point hit home. "Maybe so."

"So the stunt boss rigged the stunt?" she asked, nudging him back to that fateful day.

"Yes, the stunt boss rigged it while I was in costuming. I was in the stunt, too. By the time I got out of wardrobe and makeup, the thing was a 'go' and I wasn't given even a minute to check it." He paused, thinking back, remembering details he'd tried to forget. "It was complicated. Two-car chase scene. Alex was in the first car, and I was in the second on a bridge. A section of the bridge was out. Alex was to jump from the car and roll to safety while the cars crash and tumble through the hole in the bridge and into the water below."

"Sounds dangerous," Killian said, caught up in the story.

"Well, it was, but I'd worked it out carefully. I'd gone over it and over it with Donohugh—Bill Donohugh, the stunt boss—and Alex. The key was a spring-loaded ejection seat that would give the driver a little boost out of the seat, throwing Alex to safety." The numbness of time began to fade and the pain of yesterday pricked his heart, making his nerve ends tingle. "It worked like a charm five times, but the last time it only ejected Alex part-way. I wanted to check it out thoroughly before the next run-through, but the director wanted to shoot. Rain was predicted for later that day. Donohugh rigged the cars and we took our positions and went for it."

Killian chewed her lower lip fretfully, wanting to throw her arms around Gus; she wanted to let her imagination fill in the rest of the story, but she sensed that he needed to go on alone, that he needed to tell her everything at last. Couldn't stop him now anyway, she thought, seeing that he was past the point of no return. He was back there; back with Alex and Bill and the stunt that became his recurring nightmare.

"I didn't see much, but I saw enough." His voice sounded raw and his throat began to close as the past surrounded him, squeezed the life out of him. "The ejection seat didn't work properly... just popped Alex half-in and half-out of the car. Alex was dragged twenty feet. Nobody could have lived through it." He closed his eyes and hot tears trailed from the corners of them and down his cheeks as the horrible scene played itself out in his mind in lurid, living color. "The blood... the smell of burning rubber and flesh... God, it was awful."

He opened his eyes. Killian stared at him, her eyes red-rimmed, her lips parted, her chest heaving. He cleared his throat, but when he spoke his voice still sounded hoarse.

"You know what the director said? I finally got out of the car I was in—seemed to take a lifetime—and the director whirled around to me and said, 'I thought you said it would work, Breedlove! This is awful. We can't use this footage.' I would have killed the bastard right then and there if the others hadn't held me off him." He had to take three deep breaths before he felt he could continue. "He said he didn't realize at the time that Alex was dead, but he must have been blind. Everybody else knew. Alex was still lying on the bridge, hadn't moved a muscle. Alex trusted me..." His voice deserted him and he rubbed the heels of his hands into his eye sockets to block out the memory of the mangled body.

Killian expelled a long sigh. "Since you knew it wasn't your fault, why didn't you testify against the stunt boss?"

"I should have. I know that now. But at the time, I was so consumed with grief—" He had to stop long enough for the sob to subside within him. Another minute ticked by before he trusted himself to speak again. Killian squeezed his knee in a show of support. "I wasn't thinking straight. I just wanted to clear out. I wanted to be by myself, away from people grilling me about the stunt and Alex and why it didn't work. It was the worst time in my life, Killian." He brought his gaze level with hers and was relieved to see steadfast loyalty shining in her true-blue eyes. "I felt as if I'd been dragged right along with Alex. I was all broken up, busted, and I couldn't see how I was going to put myself back together again. I sure couldn't do it with everybody asking questions and looking to lay the blame. Since I already blamed myself, I didn't give a damn at the time if everybody else blamed me, too."

"You and Alex were good friends," Killian said, beginning to understand the depth of his pain. "I mean, you were more than just a couple of stuntmen working together. I get the feeling you were real close to him."

He took a deep, chest-expanding breath. "Alex wasn't a stuntman, Killian—"

She gasped. "Then what was he doing—"

"Alex was a stuntwoman," he said, effectively silencing Killian. "The best in the business." He cleared his throat nervously, self-consciously. "And I was in love with her. I was going to marry her."

11

GUS TOUCHED KILLIAN'S FACE with tender fingertips as if he were afraid she might crack. "From your glazed eyes, I'd say I've taken you by surprise." But he looked as glassy-eyed as she did.

"Y-yes." Killian swiped at her face as if drawing away imaginary cobwebs. "You loved Alex." She listened to that before its significance made itself felt in her heart. Examining the tragedy through his eyes, she began to understand his reluctance to talk about the accident. He'd been in love with the woman, she told herself again, and tried to ignore the pang in her heart. "That explains a lot."

"It does?" he asked, slouching on the couch, depleted.

"I thought your behavior was extreme, but to see a lover killed that way..." She shook her head, tears of pity welling up in her eyes. "After such a horrible experience, I wouldn't want to answer a bunch of questions, either. But I'm glad the investigation cleared you."

"Did it?"

"Of course." She wiped the tears from her eyes, irritated with Gus for reverting to his belief that others can't forgive or forget. "Gus, you don't really think anybody

of importance believed you would have been careless
with the life of the woman you loved."

He covered the lower part of his face with one hand—
a gesture Killian had come to recognize. His mask, Killian thought. He draped his hand from nose to chin when
he blocked out the world. Anger burned the edges of her
pity, lit by Gus's camouflage.

"I could tell early on that you were supersensitive to
any question that might have impugned your honor, and
that's endearing—to a point." She knee-walked to the
couch, but he avoided her searching gaze. Killian balled
her hands into fists and tapped his knees. "Don't shut me
out! Gus, don't you dare quit just because some strangers
might still question your integrity. I respect you. May
respects you. The people who work for you respect you.
That should be enough support for anyone."

"Yes, it should be." His voice, scratchy and raw, revealed a degree of the emotion with which he struggled,
but kept from her. He eased away from her to stand up,
stiff and unnatural. "As I've said, I'm thinking about
pulling out, but I haven't absolutely decided. I don't need
the work. I make a good living breeding horses." He tried
to smile. "And now I'm in the cattle business. Which re-
minds me, I should check on them. One of the hands was
supposed to feed them today, but I'd better—"

"Gus, we're talking here—" She snapped her teeth together, angry to be addressing his back. The screened
door flapped behind him. Killian leaped up and jogged
after him. She cautioned herself not to goad him any
further. She'd stated her case and he'd listened. The rest

was up to him. If he quit being a wrangler, she'd be disappointed in him and a little angry at him for caving in, but she'd still love him. The past few days had proved to her that her heart belonged to August Breedlove.

But did his heart belong to her, or did another woman, long dead, still guard it?

Killian rounded the corner of the barn and skidded to a halt.

"Gus? What . . . Gus?"

Gus was on his knees in the pen, a cow's head anchored in his lap. One of the cattle hadn't made it. Gus cradled it, head bent, shoulders shaking although no sound came from him. He's crying, Killian thought, alarmed, shaken to her soul. And not over some wretched cow that had been too weak to stand through another day. No, she thought, this went much farther back than that . . . back to another lost soul.

The other cattle gathered in a far corner, keeping their distance from death. Killian slipped through the wire fence and stepped gingerly toward Gus. She didn't know what she could do for him, but she knew she had to do something. After all, she was the one who had forced him to reveal the details of his past. The least she could do now was help him deal with it.

"I thought sure they'd all pull through. They seemed so much better last night and this morning. Me and Cody were out here a few minutes ago and they were all on their feet. I don't get it."

"Its heart probably gave out," Killian said. "They're so weak, Gus, it's to be expected. Their hearts are frail and their digestive systems are all messed up." She knew he already understood the frailty of his charges, but she had to say something. She studied the dead animal more carefully. "I remember this one. She was so wobbly yesterday. She was the last one to finally stand. It was too much for her, Gus. You did all you could."

Killian ran her fingers through Gus's thick hair, then leaned over to place a kiss on the crown of his head. Glistening tracks of tears striped Gus's cheeks and she felt as if her heart was breaking into jagged pieces. He wasn't thinking about the cow, but about life and death and the helplessness of mortals in a world of chance. Loss was more difficult for such a man, she thought, because he had such deep feelings and no ready outlet. A man of few words imprisoned by the shortage, Killian thought, and she felt her love for him blooming inside her, crowding out everything else.

"Sweetheart, please." Her voice crumbled, her knees buckled and she dropped to his side. She reached across, from shoulder to shoulder, to hug Gus to her. "You were alone last time, Gus, but you're not alone this time. I'll see you through, darling Gus. No matter what you decide, I'll stand by you."

He sniffed, tried to laugh. "I saw this damned cow and I . . . I was so mad! The innocent always get trampled. Why is that, Killian?"

"Easy targets for cowards, I guess," she murmured, kissing the side of his face, wishing she could do more for him. His tears tasted salty on her tongue.

"How could a man do this to a defenseless animal?" he asked, his voice hoarse, barely audible. "I look at Cody and I wonder if anything I ever told him sunk in. I thought he was a reflection of me and what I taught him, then he goes and trip-wires a horse and shows not one ounce of remorse. He just doesn't give a damn as long as he gets his payoff, his bonus, his easy money." He swallowed hard. "He apologized today."

"That's good," Killian said, grasping the ray of hope. "Isn't it? I mean, it's something."

"I guess. But he still doesn't get it. He knows right from wrong, but the line between them gets fuzzy when he sees a way to make a quick buck without breaking a sweat."

"Cody is responsible for himself," Killian said, watching the rhythmic stroking of Gus's hand on the cow's neck. The man's a romantic, but he'd never admit it, she thought. She'd never before met anyone who believed more in happy endings and did everything in his power to realize them.

"Cody knew about Alex. He knew I blamed myself for not insisting on a rehearsal. I told him over and over to go with his gut instincts even if it means rocking the boat, bucking the boss, whatever. Making a scene goes down a hell of a lot easier than living with the guilt."

Gently, Killian eased his hands from the cow and helped him to his feet. "We'll get one of your men to remove this unfortunate creature from the pen," she said. "I think the others will make it, Gus. The worst is over." Tenderly she smoothed his forehead with her fingertips and kissed his mouth lightly.

"Yes, maybe so," he said. "I hope so."

She put her arm around his waist, hooking her thumb into his belt loop, and walked slowly to the house with him. Once inside, she turned Gus toward her. "You okay?"

"Sure, I guess." He sighed, closed his eyes. "You're right. The innocent, the trusting ones are easy targets. Alex was that way. She went along. She believed. She trusted . . . me." He cleared his throat and squared his shoulders, throwing off his self-pity. "I'm sorry, Killian. About the cow, I mean. I wanted to bring them through for you."

She placed her hands on either side of his head and stood on tiptoe to look into his somber eyes. "You're still my hero, Gus. Nothing has changed that."

For an instant he looked surprised, then he made a yearning sound in his throat and his mouth swooped to hers. His fingers danced upon her face as his lips stroked hers. His tongue was a gentle suitor inside her mouth.

Killian felt his vulnerability, his blatant need for re-assurance, for comfort. She took his hands and led him to the bedroom to undress him with tender loving care. Then he returned the favor while she scattered soft, healing kisses across his eyelids, at the corners of his tempting mouth, along the stubbly ridge of his jawline.

"I love you, Gus," she whispered, and then she showed him how much she loved him.

She loved him with gentle, plucking kisses that coaxed smiles from him.

She loved him with hands that communicated trust, tenderness and adoration.

She loved him with words of passion that made little sense but said it all.

She loved him like a pledge, like a scripture, like a poem, like an anthem.

She loved him like no other.

THE NOTE read:

Dear Killian,
I know you don't like waking up alone, but I couldn't bring myself to disturb your dreams. I'd love to spend another day in bed with you, but it's Monday and I've got a long list of things to do. I know you have to go to work, too. Help yourself to coffee and biscuits in the oven.

Your hero,
Gus

"My hero," Killian said, folding the note and slipping it into her jacket pocket. She looked around the empty kitchen and into the living room. The house hadn't been what she'd expected; in fact, it was just the opposite. It was decorated very much like her own home, adding to their common ground. They weren't two peas in a pod, but they were similar in so many ways, Killian thought. More importantly, they complemented each other. He needed her to make him open up and express himself. She needed him to anchor her, give her a solid foundation and an unswerving belief in herself and what was important in her life. Is that how he saw their relationship, too? God, she hoped so.

She wandered outside, feeling like an intruder now that Gus was gone. She wished he'd awakened her. She would have liked to see his face, read his expression, hear the words he'd written. As it was, she read between the lines and decided he was probably right. The weekend was over. Monday. Blue Monday.

"Coward," she whispered, releasing a tiny bit of the bitterness she fought. "You hated to disturb my dreams? Ha! You're just not very good at mornings, Breedlove. Afternoons and evenings are your specialty."

But then, who could blame Gus if he wanted to get away and think things through? Just because she was certain of one thing—that she loved him—didn't mean he shared the same certainty. He hadn't said he loved her. Even after her confession, he'd remained mute on the subject.

"Leave him alone," she muttered to herself. "Give him time to sort things out." She climbed into her car and drove away from his ranch, but she felt as if she were leaving a part of herself behind.

She went home to change clothes and feed her animals, then broke the speed limit driving to the clinic. As it was, she was two hours late. She grimaced, knowing she was in for her father's famous sarcasm.

"Dad?" she called. "I'm here."

"I'll alert the media," came his surly response from one of the back rooms. "I'd come out and greet you, but I'm up to my ears in work. My partner didn't show this morning."

"Dad, I'm sorry." Killian went along the corridor until she spotted her father in one of the examination rooms. "There you are. Oh, hello, Dudley," she said, addressing the terrier her father was inoculating.

"Where have you been all weekend?"

"Oh, around. I was busy," she said, exchanging her lightweight jacket for a lab coat. "So, what do you want me to do first?"

"You can take care of the front while I work in surgery. I should have already been in there." He glanced at her from under his heavy, white eyebrows. "Mrs. Lawson brought Mimi in this morning for euthanasia."

"Poor Mrs. Lawson. I know that was a hard decision for her, but Mimi is . . . was?" She waited for her father's nod, telling her that the procedure was over. "She was sixteen and in so much pain from her arthritis. I hope you told Mrs. Lawson that."

"I did, but it should have been you. She wanted to talk to you, not me."

Killian glanced up at the fluorescent light fixture. "Dad, please don't go on—"

"When you take over this place I won't be around to make excuses for you. You'll have to confront these people yourself and—"

"Dad, please!" A few moments later Killian realized she'd planted her hands over her ears and had squeezed her eyes shut. When she opened her eyes, her father was staring at her as if she were a woman who was ready for a rubber room and a straitjacket. "I'm sorry for yelling that way."

"I should hope so. What's gotten into you? You drag in here three hours late—"

"Two hours."

"—without any explanation, thinking you can throw on a lab coat and let bygones be bygones—"

"Not likely, right?" she cut in, letting loose with the sarcasm she'd learned from him.

"—and then you yell at me as if I'm deaf. What's wrong with you lately? Did that Gus fellow make you forget what's important in life?"

"No, Daddy." She propped her hands at her hips and tipped her head to one side, struck by a fundamental truth. "That Gus fellow made me realize what *is* important."

"Meaning?" her father asked, placing Dudley in a carrier and closing its door with a snap.

"Meaning this clinic is not my top priority."

"This clinic won't run itself."

"No, but it's not my whole life, Daddy. I'm not you. I'm not going to marry this clinic and allow it to dictate my life and the way I live it. This clinic is only part of me." The words flowed from her heart, unstoppable, flooding past her lips. "I've tried to understand how it was with you, Daddy. How you threw yourself into your work after Mama died. How this clinic became your world. It wasn't easy, but I tried."

"When you run a business, you take on responsibilities," he said, propping his knuckles on the stainless steel table that separated him from Killian.

"When you marry and have children you also take on responsibilities," she told him. "And every person has to set his own priorities. You decided the clinic came first. Well, that's not for me. I want a husband. I want children. They will be my priorities. Then the clinic and my other work with the humane society and animal rights groups. I didn't beg forgiveness for being late this morning because I'm not at all sorry about it. Some things are more important to me than Mrs. Lawson and Mimi."

"So you'll hire someone to take up the slack," her father said, a slur in his voice. "It looks as if I've built up this business only for you to turn it over to a stranger while you chase your dreams. You're going to let my dream slip through your fingers. You'll lose this clinic. You'll ruin this business."

"No, I won't." She came around the table to grip his upper arms in a tangible appeal. "Daddy, just because I want a private life doesn't mean I'm going to destroy this business. You're not the only one who has added to the client list. I've done my part."

"Yes, that's true." He eyed her curiously. "You sound as if you resent the time I've spent building up the clinic."

"At times, I have. I can't remember a holiday that we didn't end up here checking on the animals. It seems that every one of my birthdays was interrupted by you running off to perform emergency surgery. *I* wanted to be the most important thing in your life, Daddy. Just once, I used to say to myself. Just once let it be me." Emotion choked her for a few moments and she looked away, sensing his dawning awareness.

"Killy, you must know how much I love you. I never meant to hurt you or make you feel as if—"

"I know, Daddy." She spread her hands on the front of his white coat and smiled up into his eyes. "I'm not blaming you. I understand now that you had to do things your way. But, Daddy, you have to understand that I must do things my way. And my way is different from yours. I love the clinic and I'm proud of it. I'm pleased to take it over someday. I want it to continue to be a success, to continue to serve the needs of this area."

"That's good to hear," her father said with great relief.

Killian gripped his lapels. "But the clinic can't love me back, Daddy, and I want to be loved. I want to be someone's priority and I want someone to be mine. I need that in my life."

"Have you found that someone?"

She closed her eyes and rested her cheek briefly against her father's chest. His arms came around to hold her. "I hope so, Daddy," she whispered. "With all my heart, I hope so."

"August Breedlove?"

She nodded.

"Does he love you?"

"I don't know." She spun away, seized by frustration. "He hasn't said so, but I think he does. I just wish he'd say it, you know? I need to hear it."

"Did you tell him you love him?"

"Yes. This morning he . . . well, I suppose he needed to be alone. I can understand that. Things . . . progressed pretty quickly this weekend and I guess his head is spinning like a top."

"But you're sure yours is on straight."

Killian faced her father again. "I'm positive. I think I've loved him from the moment I met him, Daddy. Sounds impossible, but it happened. I looked at the man and something inside of me fell into place. Through all the problems and fights and aggravation, my esteem for him never faltered."

"Sounds like the real McCoy to me. I fell hard and fast for your mother. I wanted to ask her to marry me on our second date, but I was afraid she'd think I was a hard-up case and it would scare her off. So I waited." He gave a sly wink. "Asked her on the third date."

"And what did she say?" Killian asked, smiling.

"She said, 'What took you so long?'"

Killian laughed. "Oh, if only it would be that simple for me and Gus." She paused, recalling things he'd said about himself. "He's a recluse, you see. You know how I like to be alone sometimes?"

"Too much of the time," her father said, his tone gently scolding.

"Yes, you're probably right. Gus is worse than me, I think. He's been a loner for a long time and he's told me that he likes it that way. I figured he needed time to be by himself and—" She stopped herself, laughing at her explanation. "Listen to me trying to justify it to myself."

"What happened?" her father asked, folding his arms across his chest in a patient gesture. "Did he say something to hurt your feelings?"

"No, worse. He left a note." She waved a careless hand. "A woman can't talk to her father about these things, Daddy."

"Not a Dear Jane note?"

"No, not exactly." She struggled to find a delicate way to put it. "Just a note...a note instead of a morning kiss. I decided he was trying to tell me that it was Monday, the weekend was over, and we should cool it."

"Killian!"

She reached out to him and felt herself blush. Talking to her own father about spending the night with a man— she must be out of her mind! "Daddy, I shouldn't have told you—"

"You're in a stew over a note? Is the man a cowboy or a writer?"

"A—a cowboy."

"Then don't put too much stock in that note, honey. As a rule, the average man can barely compose a shopping list without screwing it up. So he got up early, left a note, and then went about his business. That doesn't mean he doesn't expect to have you back in his arms come sundown."

"You—you think so?" she asked, almost afraid to believe him.

"I know so. He's got a ranch to run, doesn't he?"

"Yes."

"Well, he sure can't run it from bed. No more than you can run this clinic from one."

She felt her blush deepen as she kissed her father's lined cheek. "I never thought I'd talk to you about such things."

"I hope you can talk to me about anything."

She stood back, seeing her father clearly, albeit through the rose-colored glasses of love. "I'm lucky to have you." She placed an arm around his shoulders. "You know, if I hire a junior partner, it would give me a little more freedom. I could buy a travel trailer and take a trip with you once in awhile."

He angled back to give her the eagle eye. "You mean it?"

"Yes, I mean it. I love to see new places." She laughed at his sudden frown. "What's got you down-in-the-mouth?"

"Awww, you and this wrangler will probably get married and then you won't want to go anywhere with your old man."

"Don't bet on it. The wrangler can go with us, can't he?"

"You think he'll like trailers? Most folks want to go by air and stay in motels or hotels."

Killian laughed again, remembering a rainy night, a roadside motel and a certain horse trailer. "Daddy, the man is crazy about trailers. Loves to sleep in them. He'd trade a motel room for a trailer."

Her father nodded gravely. "I approve." He eyed her carefully again. "You want to work or would you rather go home and chart your next ambush of this doomed bachelor?"

"I'd rather work," she assured him. "If he wants me, he knows where to find me."

"Atta girl. Make him give chase. Men love a good hunt."

SHE HELD OUT until quitting time, then she drove home to shower and change clothes before driving straight to Gus's ranch. She'd stewed all day, wondering if he loved her or if he was anywhere close to feeling that way. Then she decided she had a right to know. When she was in bed with him, she didn't doubt it. But that note...that blasted note! If only he'd signed it "Love, Gus." That would have eased her tortured heart.

"He can say the words," she muttered darkly, steering her car onto his property. "He must have said them to Alex. After all, they were going to marry! Well, he can damn well say them to me or I'm out of here. I'm too old and too ornery to play house. I want the real thing!"

She bounded out of the car, slamming the door and plodding purposefully to the house when she realized Gus was standing off to one side near his pickup, hat in one hand, keys in the other.

"You going somewhere?" she asked, swerving toward him. "I won't keep you long," she said, not wanting to give him a chance to dodge her.

"Would you come—"

"No, I can't come back later. I have to talk to you now. Right this instant," she barked, realizing she must have sounded like a drill sergeant, but unable to soften her tone. He was too cute for words and she was afraid she'd weaken if she let him say much.

"Let me put on—"

"No, don't go to any trouble," she interrupted, not wanting him to put on coffee or tea or any other beverage. "Gus, I understand that you need to be alone. You told me that once and I remember it."

"Right, and I've cha—"

"Please, Gus, let me finish." She issued a stern glare that silenced him. He nodded, giving her the floor. "When I read your note this morning, I figured you wanted time alone to think, so I've given you that time. But I need to know where I stand with you. I hate to put you on the spot, but I'm afraid I've fallen in love with you and if the feeling isn't mutual, well...I wouldn't want to stick around." She sucked in a deep breath, needing fortification. "You loved Alex, right?"

He started to answer, paused, then raised his dark eyebrows questioningly. "May I answer?"

"Yes, of course," she said, irritated that he wasn't completely serious.

"Yes, I loved Alex."

"Then you told her as much?"

"Yes, I told her."

"That's good, because a woman needs to know. Whatever you feel toward me, share it with me." She wagged her head from side to side, anticipating his irritation. "I know, there's that word you hate so much. Share. But that's what love is to me, Gus. It's sharing. I don't want any mysteries between me and the man I love. They don't tantalize me, they make me feel insecure."

"We can't have that."

"And—another thing—this way you have of grinning at me when I'm trying to be serious."

"But you're so cute."

"Gus!" She stamped one foot and stared blindly at the ground, desperate to make him understand how wretched she felt.

"I love you."

Her head came up. "Wh-what?"

"You heard me. I love you." He made a throwaway gesture with the hand holding his hat. "There. It's not hard for me to say."

"It's not?" She felt as if she'd run a mile for no good reason. Her heart beat double time and she experienced a moment of dizziness.

"No, it's not." He reached through the open window of his pickup and pulled out a small sack. "Look what I found at the five-and-ten." He handed her a ring. "Know what that is?"

Taking it from him, she examined the piece of costume jewelry, then laughed. "It's a mood ring."

"You're not the only one who's been listening and filing away bits and pieces of conversations." He leaned against the body of the truck and crossed his ankles and arms. "But let's not take this too far."

"Take . . . what?" She slipped the ring onto her index finger and trembled inside. Oh, God. Here it comes. He's going to say that he loves me, but not enough to let me all the way into his life. Then I'm going to have to tell him *adios* because I can't live in the shadow of love.

"Let's not chisel every little thing we've said to each other in granite," he explained.

"Oh. Yes. I . . . see." She had trouble getting the words out, pushing them past her numb lips, one by one. Forget the sweet talk, she translated for him. Don't hold him to the magical things he said to you. You know better than to believe pillow talk; only a fool takes to heart what's said between the sheets.

"Since meeting you, I've undergone some changes. I don't love being alone as much as I used to," he said, throwing her another curve.

"Oh?" Hope nudged her heart.

"You ruined it for me." He smiled, then forced a scowl to his face. "Sorry. I forgot that you don't like my smile."

"No . . . no!" She reached out to him, laughing at his teasing. How he could tease her when her heart was on the verge of either breaking or soaring way beyond her. "That's not what I meant. I love your smile."

"Good." He sighed as if relieved of a burden, then beamed. "Because you make me smile, Killy. You make me laugh and love and want to be with you all the time."

He wasn't teasing. He was serious. Heavenly day! She couldn't stand it any longer. In a split second, she was in his arms, rubbing her cheek against the front of his shirt, back where she belonged. An odd chord sounded in her head. *Killy.* Killy?

"You called me Killy," she said, raising her head to look at him.

"That's what your dad calls you." He nodded, confirming her suspicions. "I talked to him."

"When?" she asked, looking at his truck. A pinging sounded under the hood. Metal cooling, she realized. He'd already been somewhere. He wasn't on his way out as she'd thought at first.

"Just now. I stopped by the clinic, thought I'd catch you before you left work, but you'd already headed home."

"Daddy was still there?" she asked, dreading his answer. What in the world had Daddy said to him? she wondered, then wondered if she really wanted to know. Men said women were great gossips, but she knew that two men could put two women to shame in that department any day of the week.

"Your dad and I had a fine old talk about our favorite person in the whole world." His arms tightened. "You. Don't mind if another adoring male calls you Killy every once in awhile, do you?"

"No, not at all." His face blurred as tears built in her eyes. Never in her wildest dreams had she imagined she could love a man this much.

"I didn't need to get away from you to think," he admonished. "I needed to plan."

"Plan?" She ran her hands across his shoulders where fancy stitching created a vee design. The heat of his skin seeped through the cotton shirt.

"Plan," he repeated. "I had to go to the bank and then pick up a few things today. That mood ring for one."

"Oh, yes. This is highly important." She glanced at it. "It's blue. That means I'm happy, I think."

"You don't know?"

"Yes, I know. I'm happy." She wound her fingers in the curls at the nape of his neck. "What else did you pick up? Something for dinner?" she asked, making a few plans of her own. Him in bed, then dinner, then him in bed again and again and again.

"Dinner?" He made a scoffing sound. "Nothing that boring." He gently pulled her arms away from him and tossed his hat and keys onto the seat of the truck. Then he reached into his back pocket for a small, black box. "Know what this is? Don't open it unless you're willing to accept it," he warned. "Let me down easy."

She stared at the box, knowing full well it held her future. "Gus, I thought you were working all day."

"Working? After last night?" He chuckled at such an idea. "After what we did to each other—for each other— I couldn't think of anything but you. I didn't want to spend another night wondering if it might be my last one with you."

"You mean, you were . . ." She laughed, finding the whole scenario too pitiful for words. "Are we a couple of insecure lovesick fools or what?"

"I know you believe in me," he said, his lips grazing her forehead. "And that means the world to me. It took me a while to trust my good fortune—that a woman of your compassion, desirability and beauty could love a stubborn, broken-up wrangler like me."

"Oh, Gus, you're so much more than that to me," she said, filling her eyes with him, clutching the tiny box he'd given her.

"I'm not broken anymore, Killian. Your love, your faith healed me. I'm not a quitter anymore and, if you hadn't noticed before now, I'm not running anywhere. I'm staying put and I want you to stay with me. I want you in my life from here on in, Killian. Will you open that box and let me slide that ring onto your finger?"

She opened it. The lid creaked. A ray of sunshine shattered itself in the prisms of the emerald-cut diamond set in rich, warm gold.

"You know what they say," Gus whispered. "A diamond is forever." He worked the band from the casing and slipped the ring onto her appropriate finger. "Fits. I knew it would."

"It's beautiful," she said, amazed she could get that much past the lump in her throat. A teardrop slipped off her cheek and splashed onto the diamond, christening it with her love.

"I hope you're crying out of pure joy and not because you think that ring is the ugliest thing you ever laid eyes on," he said with a sigh.

"Hush your mouth!" she scolded. "This happens to be the ring I've always dreamed of, ever since I was twelve and looking through *Brides* magazine, I'll have you know!" She tipped her head to one side as curiosity arrested her. "How did you know, by the way?"

"Lucky Gus." He winked slyly. "That's what folks used to call me. Looks like my luck is back, sweetheart."

"Looks like it." She pulled his head down for a heartfelt kiss. "Gus, let's go inside."

"In a minute. Come here." He draped his arm around her shoulders and set off in the direction of the barn. Arabians and Morgans tossed their proud heads and whinnied when they spotted him.

"Look at those horses," Killian said, so full of joy that everything around her seemed bigger than life, brighter than the sun. "They're calling out to you, wanting you to notice them. You have such a way with animals, Gus."

"And with you, I hope."

"You know you do."

"Look, Killian. Doesn't that make you feel good inside?"

She followed his gaze to the cattle in the pen. They all chomped busily, feeding on grain, some standing, some lying down while they chewed on their cud.

"Gus, they look so much better," she said, moving to the fence for a closer inspection. "The sores are healing and just look at them eat!" She whirled to face him again. "It's a miracle!"

"We're a miracle."

Tears sprang to her eyes again. "Yes, we are."

He turned her around to face the pasture and crossed his arms over her, holding her tightly against him. "See that land, Killian?"

"It's beautiful land."

"It needs you almost as much as I do. This land was meant for a family, not a crusty bachelor full of sour grapes." His lips pressed a warm kiss to her temple. "Until I met you it seemed that every time I was close to happiness, it crumbled in my hands like diamonds to dust."

She looked at the diamond he'd given her, at how it sparkled in the sun and gave off the light of hope. Grasping his hands, she held them in front of her to admire them. "These hands?" she asked. "These hands turned diamonds to dust?"

"Yes," he said, a smile coloring his voice.

Killian turned around to feast upon his smile. She took one of his hands and placed it on her hip. The other, she pressed against the side of her face. His eyes made her think of melting chocolate, liquid temptation. "You're wrong, August Breedlove. The magic is in these hands. Magic in your touch."

His mouth courted hers and a divine warmth spread throughout her. She caught fire and caught him up in it.

The diamond sparkled as her hand stroked and caressed the man she loved, and the globe on her other ring changed to purple. Passionate purple.

HARLEQUIN Temptation

Lovers Apart

FOUR CONTROVERSIAL STORIES! FOUR DYNAMITE AUTHORS!

Don't miss the LOVERS APART miniseries—four special Temptation books. Look for the third book and the subsequent titles listed below:

March: **Title #340**
MAKING IT by Elise Title

Hannah and Marc . . . Can a newlywed yuppie couple—both partners having demanding careers—find "time" for love?

April: **Title #344**
YOUR PLACE OR MINE by Vicki Lewis Thompson

Lila and Bill . . . A divorcée and a widower share a shipboard romance but they're too set in their ways to survive on land!

If you missed January title #332—DIFFERENT WORLDS by Elaine K. Stirling and February title #336—DÉTENTE by Emma Jane Spenser and would like to order them, send your name, address, and zip or postal code, along with a check or money order for $2.65 plus 75¢ postage and handling ($1.00 in Canada) for each book ordered, payable to Harlequin Reader Service, to:

In the U.S.
3010 Walden Ave.
Box 1325
Buffalo, NY 14269-1325

In Canada
P.O. Box 609
Fort Erie, Ontario
L2A 5X3

Please specify book title(s) with your order.
Canadian residents please add applicable federal and provincial taxes.

LAP-3

HARLEQUIN
Romance®

This March, travel to Australia with Harlequin Romance's FIRST CLASS title #3110 FAIR TRIAL by Elizabeth Duke.

They came from two different worlds.

Although she'd grown up with a privileged background, Australian lawyer Tanya Barrington had worked hard to gain her qualifications and establish a successful career.

It was unfortunate that she and arrogant barrister Simon Devlin had to work together on a case. He had no time for wealthy socialites, he quickly informed her. Or for women who didn't feel at home in the bush where he lived at every available opportunity. And where he had Tanya meet him to discuss the case.

Their clashes were inevitable—but their attractions to each other was certainly undeniable. . . .

Take 4 bestselling love stories FREE

Plus get a FREE surprise gift!

Coming in March from

HARLEQUIN®

LaVyrle Spencer's unforgettable story of a
love that wouldn't die.

LaVyrle Spencer

SWEET MEMORIES

She was as innocent as she was unsure . . . until a very special
man dared to unleash the butterfly wrapped in her cocoon and
open Teresa's eyes and heart to love.

SWEET MEMORIES is a love story to savor that will make you
laugh—and cry—as it brings warmth and magic into your
heart.

"Spencer's characters take on the richness of friends, relatives
and acquaintances.''   —*Rocky Mountain News*

SWEET

COMING IN 1991 FROM
HARLEQUIN SUPERROMANCE:

Three abandoned orphans,
one missing heiress!

Dying millionaire Owen Byrnside receives an
anonymous letter informing him that twenty-six years
ago, his son, Christopher, fathered a daughter. The
infant was abandoned at a foundling home that
subsequently burned to the ground, destroying all
records. Three young women could be Owen's long-
lost granddaughter, and Owen is determined to track
down each of them! Read their stories in

#434 HIGH STAKES (available January 1991)
#438 DARK WATERS (available February 1991)
#442 BRIGHT SECRETS (available March 1991)

Three exciting stories of intrigue and romance by
veteran Superromance author Jane Silverwood.

Everyone loves a spring wedding, and this April,
Harlequin cordially invites you to read the most
romantic wedding book of the year.

ONE WEDDING—FOUR LOVE STORIES
FROM OUR MOST DISTINGUISHED
HARLEQUIN AUTHORS:

BETHANY CAMPBELL
BARBARA DELINSKY
BOBBY HUTCHINSON
ANN McALLISTER

*The church is booked, the reception arranged and the
invitations mailed. All Diane Bauer and Nick Granatelli
have to do is walk down the aisle. Little do they realize that
the most cherished day of their lives will spark so many
romantic notions....*

Available wherever Harlequin books are sold. HWED-1AR